As Close As You'll Ever Be

stories by
Seamus Scanlon

CAIRN
PRESS

Cairn Press LLC

Cairn Press LLC
www.cairnpress.com

Cover photo by Cristina Kotz Cornejo © 2012
Book layout by Jesse Blodgett
Author photo by Maria Providencia Casanovas © 2012
Editors: Joshua Daniel Cochran, Jody Thompson

Cairn Press LLC
405 Wetmore Road
#117-146
Tucson, Arizona 85705

First edition, August 2012
ISBN-13: 978-0985319717
Printed in the United States.

*This is a work of fiction. Real places and events have been changed and
fictionalized. All characters are of the author's imagination and any resemblance to actual persons, living or dead, is entirely coincidental.*

Contents

The following stories are award winners or have been previously published:

"The Long Wet Grass," won the 2011 Fish One-Page Prize and was first published in *The Fish Anthology, 2011*.

"Teenage Sniper" was published in *The Lineup 3* (2010).

"The Butterfly Love Song" won the 2010 Over The Edge New Writer of the Year Contest and was published as "Lucy Block Waited" in *The Review of Post Graduate English Studies* (2011).

Portions of "Infected" were published in *Promethean 37*, 2010, under the title "Galway über Alles."

"Remember" was published in part in *The Review of Post Graduate English Studies* (2004).

"Collecting" was published in *Crimespree Magazine* (2012).

"No Exceptions" was published in *The Crime Factory* under the title "House of Pain" (2012).

"My Beautiful, Brash, Beastly Belfast," won the 2011 *Gemini Magazine* Short Story Contest and was published online (2011).

To Hugo Kelly
Thanks Very Much

As Close As You'll Ever Be

Best Wishes

Seán
Aug '13 Galway

The Long Wet Grass

The resonance of tires against the wet road is a mantra strong and steady. The wipers slough rain away in slow rhythmic arcs into the surrounding blackness. The rain falls slow and steady, then gusting, reminding me of Galway when I was a child where Atlantic winds flung broken fronds of seaweed onto the Prom during high tide. Before the death harmony of Belfast seduced me.

The wind keeps trying to tailgate us. But we keep sailing. The slick-black asphalt sings on beneath us. We slow and turn onto a dirt road, the clean rhythm now broken, high beams tracing tall reeds edging against the road moving rhythmically back and forth with the wind. No lights now from oncoming cars.

We stop at a clearing. I open the door. The driver looks back at me. The rain on my face is soothing. The pungent petrol fumes comfort me. The moon lies hidden behind black heavy clouds. I unlock the trunk.

You can barely stand after lying curled up for hours. After a while you can stand straight. I take the tape from your mouth. You breathe in the fresh air. You breathe in the fumes. You watch me. You don't beg. You don't cry. You are brave.

I hold your arm and lead you away from the roadway, into a field, away from the car, from the others. The pistol in my hand pointed at the ground. I stop. I kiss your cheek. I raise the pistol. I shoot you twice high in the temple. The coronas of light anoint you. You fall. The rain rushes to wipe the blood off. I fire shots into the air. The ejected shells skip away.

I walk back to the car and leave you there lying in the long wet grass.

Rob

My brother Rob read books on anatomy while still in high school. He was a high achiever. He showed me pictures of knife wounds, hangings, amputations, diseased hearts and cancer-tainted lungs.

"Don't fucking smoke, okay?" he warned me.

I didn't mind the pictures, but hated the smell of the books. I felt they had been resting on mortuary and dissection tables and were steeped in countless viruses and other pathogens yet undiscovered.

"Jesus, will you look at those fucking brain tumors," he would say. "Fuck me."

He took these books from the university's medical library by breaking in at night. It was reported in the *Galway Advertiser*. I cut out the story and kept it with the collection of books on the Viet Cong and mnemonics that he stole for me. He was a bibliophile burglar. I waited for him in Court House Square while he climbed the trees beside the library and jumped from a branch onto the roof. When he came down, we ran through the streets in the cold early morning like junior ninjas. During the summer holidays he worked in the incinerator room of the Regional Hospital where body parts were flung into the flames after surgeries. And oblivion. It was the oblivion he wanted in his own life but didn't achieve until much later.

Our housing estate was as tough as the cold, rough concrete walls of the houses. The Rattlesnakes patrolled the local streets and sometimes filled them with blood. They struck like Saracen cavalry rushing from concealed positions. I often felt they could outrun victims easily but maintained their distance to cause the maximum stress. The Rattlesnakes were sallow, suntanned and muscular. They looked like Apaches. But real Apaches were more merciful than our indigenous variety. We kept running until our sides hurt and all traces of self-esteem were gone. When they caught us we fought like the damned, which we were. They fought us wordlessly and breathlessly and gracefully and instinctively like primitive gifted urban warriors. The Rattlesnakes were street fighters with exhibitionist tendencies. Street fighting is primeval because it happens in an urban setting where the last thing you expect is a throwback to some primitive brain stem triggers. (I picked up some of Rob's nomenclature.) They were skinheads who wore Doc Martens, parallels, and carried girls on their arms and knives in ankle sheaths and patrolled the streets with Alsatians. They looked striking, and that's what they did. I admired their ruthlessness, their swagger, their ease in their bodies. And especially their girls.

In addition to gross anatomy, Rob studied forensic pathology, forensic psychology, and other related subjects such as morgue etiquette in his spare time. He rarely spoke. He was examined by the school psychologist but had mastered the DSM classifications by heart so he excelled during the one hour session allotted by the school. They need to improve those tests or at least the testers.

Once Rob graduated high school, where his intense intellectual fire had begun to scorch synapses, he passed the entrance interview and exams and went to medical school. We had to keep it quiet. Even my mother recognized the danger of leaking this. He had to pretend to the Rattlesnakes that he still worked in the hospital incinerator room. College attendance and professional careers were frowned upon and if they suspected you deviated from the manual labor or criminal career path, you were set upon. Instead, there was positive discrimination in favor of street fighting, mugging and joy riding. They stopped Rob in the street and would ask, "So you still up in the fucking Regional?" while an Alsatian sniffed at his legs.

"Yes."

"What's it like?"

"Good."

They would laugh.

"Any chance you could get me a start there?"

"I'll ask."

But he never did and they didn't expect it.

"Okay. See you, Doc."

They all laughed and ran up the road, their metal tipped boots ringing against the wet pavement, their Alsatians running like Cuchulainn's hounds, parallels flapping, their skinhead girlfriends running by their sides, eyes ahead, fixed, content in their own pursuit of physicality and oblivion.

When I was eleven and my brother sixteen, I went with him to finish a fight that started in school. I had never seen him so agitated. I was unnerved because it was out of character. He didn't want me to come, but I insisted. I walked into the bedroom and he was getting ready to go out.

"Where you going?"

"Nowhere."

"Nowhere where?"

"Never mind."

"Never mind never mind. Where?"

"Not far."

"How far is not far?"

"Jesus, you should be a fucking cop."

"Cop off. Where you going?"

He told me.

One of his classmates had called him a homo.

"Fuck him," I said.

"Exactly. That's what I'm going to do."

"No, I mean fuck him as in forget him. Who cares?"

"I care."

"I mean it's not worth it."

"Sometimes it's worth it."

Fuck me, I wasn't getting anywhere.

He looked out the window.

"We'll wait till later," he said. "Too bright still." He hunkered down on the floor with his back to the wall, his coat on, and hummed to himself. He reached up and flicked the light off. After an hour, when it was dark out, he stood up. "Okay," he said.

We left via the back garden. He carried a grudge that wouldn't budge and I carried the worry of him getting caught and losing him. If he did, I'd be flying on my own. Really, I was only there as a self-appointed restraining influence. Rob was good at anatomy, algebra, differentiation, even integration, just not the social kind. I wanted to prevent the street fighting version of the Hindenburg disaster if I could.

We walked down to the end of the garden and out the wooden gate. There was a laneway behind the houses which would minimize our exposure to the neighbors, but it was raining heavily so the streets were deserted. We stopped briefly to look at the shadow of a girl studying in an upstairs bedroom. He gazed upward for about five minutes. I didn't say anything because I thought she might distract him and, hopefully, make him abandon the mission. I just let the rain run down my neck and waited. And hoped for the best.

"You see her?" he eventually said.

"Yeah."

I thought he was going to remark on her mammary glands (I had a big vocabulary for a sawn-off kid) or similar since these were the only type of comments I heard from boys at school about girls. I knew she was an American who moved to Galway with her parents and was in Rob's class.

"She's beautiful," he said.

Pause.

"She's a real bright spark," he added.

After another pause he looked at me.

"Someday she might talk to me."

Jesus. Romeo lives, I thought.

"Let's go," he said. I looked up for the last time and tried to visualize a girl with breasts and brains. It was a lot to comprehend.

We kept going until we got to the end of the back gardens and watched the road to ensure there was no traffic and then ran in a crouch to another alley on an adjacent avenue. When we got to the house of his tormenter, I asked "are you sure?" He nodded. I followed him up the garden path in more ways than one. He knocked at the door and there was movement inside the kitchen and then we heard a key turning in the lock.

The father of the accused answered the door. He looked a bit frightened but when he saw me he relaxed. How much damage could I do? It was dark. We were only shadows. The light streaming out from the back door highlighted the rain streaming down in steady sheets. We wiped rain from our eyes.

"What are you doing at the back door?"

"We tried the front door and there was no answer."

"Okay, what is it?"

"Is Tim in?"

Rob had nicknamed Tim 'Frog-Face' because of his looks. I could see where he got them.

"He can't be disturbed."

"Can I see him just for a second? It's about homework."

"No, I'm afraid you can't. It will have to do tomorrow. Can I give him a message?"

There was a pause as my brother considered this.

"Yes, you can give him this."

Rob turned sideways to get the maximum force into his delivery and, with both hands grasping the handle, swung the hatchet he had carried from our house unbeknownst to me in a wide arc into Daddy Frog-Face's froghead. He used so much force the blade stuck in the skull. Rob tried to pull the hatchet free but couldn't. Eventually, the man fell to his knees and kept falling to the wet path and pulled Rob down as well. Whatever awkward way he toppled, Rob ended up trapped beneath him. I was sort of whimpering at this stage. I was hoping Rob's knowledge of anatomy would have guided his blow to produce the maximum terror and the minimum damage but he must have panicked or else it never even occurred to him. I always thought I knew what he was thinking but since he rarely spoke I had to make assumptions.

From under the fallen father I did free him.

"Jesus, how thick is this guy's head?" Rob asked. "It's stuck solid. I can't budge it."

Stuck fuck, I thought. I shrugged my shoulders.

He laid the man on his back and had to stand on his chest to finally pull the blade free. Nobody came to the back door which was a minor miracle since we were making a lot of noise. Tim must have been studying his arse off.

"He's not dead," Rob said as he became pallid. He was sweating and shaking. I knew I had to take control. I knelt down close beside the axee so I could see for myself.

"He's as close as he'll ever be," I said.

I had to pull Rob to make him move. He kept saying, "Jesus, Jesus, Jesus." I was saying the same, but for a different reason.

"Rob, pull yourself together."

Rob was getting panicky. He looked like a case of shell shock. If we were on the front line of World War I, he would have been shot at dawn. I linked his arm to guide him home. This was the new me. On the way back, we kept to the alleys and only stopped for a few minutes outside the American girl's house. He stared up at the room and shivered from the cold and the shock.

"Come on you fucking eejit," I said.

We didn't sleep very well that night. Every time I closed my eyes, the fear in Frog-Face's father's face I did see. My brother lay on top of the bed with the hatchet in his hands like a medieval prince clutching a crosier on top of an ornate casket. We washed the hatchet on the way back so there were no stains in the bedroom. I could not pull the hatchet out of Rob's hands so I left it. The moonlight shone off the blade during the night.

Just before dawn, Rob fell asleep. I took the hatchet and put it under the bed when I heard my mother coming up the stairs. I placed his copy of *Skin Diseases Through the Ages* on his chest. My mother looked in and said nothing. I feigned sleep. She glanced at the top of the wardrobe from where I jumped onto the bed every night but had never caught me in the act. I felt she was trying to reconstruct the arcs and vectors of my flights from looking at the launch pad. She closed the door and I lay awake for a few hours thinking of free-falling, hatchets and the girl silhouetted in the window. We got up late and didn't speak about the previous evening. I flew off the wardrobe for a while and my brother read.

We listened to the *RTE Morning News* about the assault and learned that Daddy Frog-Face was still alive. He wasn't as close as I thought.

"That fucker has the thickest skull in history if you ask me," I said to Rob.

We learned that the axee would make a full recovery and luckily enough had amnesia. He didn't know us to see in any event, but it was risky. Rob looked at me during the broadcast. He was in shock. He never expected the reality to be so disturbing. I could see his relief by the reprieve. It redoubled his conviction to study forensic pathology and to further isolate himself from social interaction.

A few days later the Gardaí visited the school and spoke with all Frog-Face's classmates, including Rob. After the school psychologist's examination, the local police were no problem. Rob had regained his composure and gave an alibi—he was at home with me and our mother all night. When they called to the house, I presumed it was some unwanted guest so I ran through the house on my tidying streak without her even telling me. When she did call me downstairs, she looked worried and said there were two detectives to talk to me and not to worry, she would be there.

"Hi sonny," the older red-haired Garda said when I came into the sitting room.

"The name's Victor," I said.

He looked nonplused by the tone of my response. The other one laughed.

"Good one," the second Garda said, a young cop with bright eyes.

The older one looked at his notebook.

"I thought your name was James."

"It is, but so is Victor."

"He prefers Victor," my mother added. "It's his favorite comic."

"Jesus, weird—Okay, Victor, sit down here beside me."

"I'd rather stand if you don't mind."

"Victor sit down!" said my mother.

I sat down.

"Vic, how's school?" the red-haired one asked.

"The name's Victor," I said.

"He's a bit particular about his name," my mother apologized.

"Okay, Victor, aged eleven and a quarter, can you tell me where you were on the twelfth?"

"The twelfth of what?"

"The twelfth of this month, you little fu—" He cleared his throat. "Sorry, missus," he addressed my mother. The old guy was losing his temper.

My mother was smiling at the younger detective so missed the near expletive.

"You know. The night some crazy fu... kid attacked Mr.

10

Reck."

"I thought he had amnesia," I said.

"He did, but he remembers a few things. So where were you?"

"I was here."

"Who else was here?"

"My brother Rob and my mother."

"Are you sure?"

"Yes."

"Why are you sure?"

"Because Rob never goes out except to school and never at night."

"What about your mother?"

"What about her?"

"Does she go out?"

"You think she did it?"

"You said she was here also?" the younger Garda interrupted.

"I thought it was a kid who wrecked Mr. Reck," I said.

"Just answer the question," the older one snapped.

"My mother never goes out at night unless it's to evening classes or to lay out the dead."

"What?"

"My mother is a nurse. She helps lay out the dead for neighbors, etcetera."

"Oh."

The two of them stood up. The older one looked at me.

"No further questions."

"Should I stay in town?" I said.

"Very funny."

The younger one winked at me as they left. He also winked at my mother. Maybe it was a lazy eye, but I don't think so. The older one turned at the door.

"We might be back."

But they weren't.

Teenage Sniper

On a warm balcony floor a teenage sniper fires and the summer sun flashes against the Belfast Hills for the last time that day as the night takes aim at the lights of the city.

A soldier falls. A hollow copper-headed rifle round pierces his combat jacket, drills and spills down through his body until it can go no further.

He lies on the wet Irish road. Eyes half closed. Dark arterial blood staining the blacktop. The Belfast Hills fading slowly.

A Shotgun Kill

He kicked the door in. I integrated the sound of splintering wood into a forest scene—lightning striking a tall oak tree. I was passed out on the couch. The bed was more comfortable, but I couldn't find it the night before. My brain was uncomfortable because it couldn't kick start my body to lift my pistol.

He kicked it across the hardwood floor. It slid away like a bullet skimming water.

He kicked me in the face. The tree fell on top of me. I slid away into blackness.

He used shoes with steel toe caps. "They're your only man," they say in Ireland.

When I woke up, the barrel was pressed against my temple.

Temple Dee…

Temple Dum…

I smell the blood of an Irishman. Me.

"Do you know what you are?" he asked.

I shrugged. It hurt. A stream of black-red blood came out of my nose and mouth. I could still taste the steel through the blood. He put a lot of foot-pounds of pressure into that kick, torque-wise.

I didn't like it.

I didn't like him.

I didn't beg and I didn't falter.

After all, I killed his father.

Be worried? Maybe I oughta.

Jesus, I must have brain injuries, I thought. It doesn't even rhyme, except sorta.

"What can I do for you?" I asked.

"What can you do for me... That's a good one. You think you're so smart?"

"It has been said."

"Not by me."

"That's true."

"Well, what's your story before I blow your superior brains out the back of your skull?"

"He had it coming."

"You have it coming."

I believed him.

"He wasn't a nice guy, you know—your father."

"It doesn't matter. He was my father. That's why it matters."

"He knew the risks."

"What risks?"

"He's dead, isn't he? I'd call that high risk."

"You'll join him soon."

I believed him.

"He was taking liberties," I said.

"You're taking liberties."

"Look, he knew the score."

"He didn't deserve a sawn-off, twelve-bore."

Jesus, this sounded like a poetry slam or something. I looked up at him.

"I don't use shotguns."

"I saw the body. His head was blown off."

"I don't use shotguns. No finesse. You might as well use a bazooka while you're at it."

That's what I would use, I said, pointing to the corner of the room where the pistol glinted on the polished floor like a piece of jewelry in the half light.

He turned to look.

I pulled the sawn-off from the cushion beneath me. He

looked, but it was too late. He spun around and I pushed it under his chin.

I fired and put him in a blood-splattering tailspin.

It tore his head off.

I was nearly ill.

I think it was the drink.

Free-fall

The first time it happened I was ten. A force gripped me and flowed down my body from the top of my head. It swept me up in its energy and urgency and power. I could barely resist. I stood at the top of the stairs and knew I wanted to soar to the bottom step. I felt I could do it after all the years practicing jumping off the wardrobe onto the bed, but I hesitated.

Instead, I pushed my cousin Susan who was standing beside me. I don't remember doing it. I usually slipped in and out of a fugue state when the urge to jump was so strong. I do remember her shrieking as she flew out in a graceful arc as if to meet her guardian angel and maybe he caught her because she survived. Her supple frame was badly bruised, but no bones were broken. Fallin' Susan.

Her psychic make-up did not survive intact. As a teenager and as an adult she caused herself and her family a lot of strife. The last I heard she was training to be a female priest in an obscure offshoot of the Catholic Church.

She always avoided our house after that. And even though she went catatonic for a while, her parents didn't believe there was anything sinister in what happened. Children have accidents all the time, they declared. They were both practicing psychoanalysts, which might explain their complete lack of common sense, elementary reasoning, deduction or action. Psychoanalysts have to be certified to practice, but they should also be certified to reproduce or even exist, if you ask me.

My mother wasn't as sanguine, however, because she had seen my early special interest in falling bodies, flying, jumping, tree climbing and walking on high rooftops. Whenever I watched a TV program on dogfights, plane crashes, the history of flight, air balloons, Zeppelins and all things aeronautical, I went into a kind of stasis. A total immersion in that life and a desertion of this one. My metabolism slowed and my respiration almost stopped.

I saw my cousin Susan years later in college. She went pale and tried to avoid me, but I approached her and engaged her in friendly banter. This caused confusion and made her even more nervous. Maybe she had been mistaken all along? Surely if I was this unguarded nothing serious had occurred on that night when she and her parents came to visit our threadbare council house.

Maybe she thought I had selective amnesia or, worse still, that I was a total asocial aberration. Neither alternative was palatable. She was a bit more relaxed near the end of the encounter and I was glad. I was going to say "did you have any more free-falls lately?" but I didn't. Restraint is my middle name. After all, she had enough to cope with—her parents were still alive.

I was always interested in flight.

I had a big selection of Airfix models that I assembled, painted, and decorated with decals. Then I hung them from the ceiling of my bedroom; Sopwith Camels, Junkers, Messerschmitts, Spitfires and Zeros. I also hung plastic models of eagles, hawks and Pterodactyls. There was no way those heavy fuckers could fly, no matter what my childhood encyclopedia said.

I knew about the invention of the front mounted machine gun that fired through the rotating blades of propellers but did not hit them. I imagined the terror experienced by World War I pilots with no parachutes as their planes spiraled in flames to the ground. I had a photo of the Hindenburg airship crashing in New Jersey after its transatlantic flight from Germany as the hydrogen vapor ignited, causing the most famous and most reproduced flight disaster fire. My interest in objects plummeting to earth, or soaring above it, was genuine and all consuming and started early.

I began jumping off the wardrobe and onto the bed when I was around five. It was a big fall for a small fucker. My older brother Rob watched me from the bed as he read and made adjustments when I veered off course. He monitored me in his peripheral vision. Occasionally, he had to make vigorous efforts to get out of the way when I headed straight at him.

This sometimes happened when I used the blindfold. Once, I hit his raised knees as he lay reading and was concussed for over an hour. After Rob retrieved the book that flew across the room when I crash-landed, he resumed reading. He left me wandering around the bedroom dazed, humming nursery rhymes—and that's not me. Rob was typical doctor material. He was specializing already and hadn't even started college. He wasn't interested in physical maladies, such as childhood concussion, just the mental ones behind aerial flights like mine.

When he was in a benevolent mood, he lay on his back, bent his knees, and balanced me on the soles of his feet. I swayed there, chest supported, and held my hands wide open and imagined I was a bird of prey riding air currents. He would move his legs in circles or raise his feet up and down together. I transcended normal physical feelings and rapture overtook me. After a while he became so adept that he would keep reading with his head turned to the side to see the print while I looked down from my new aerie.

Sometimes I used the bathroom towel as a cape and pretended I was Robin. I used his TV lines like "Holy Pterodactyl!" Other times, I brushed against the light shade as I flew past so that the swinging light replicated searchlights trying to capture a marauding plane in a column of light for ack-ack gunners to bring down.

It felt great to leap from that dusty perch and crash onto

the bed. Eventually, my little body would begin to ache from all the landings and the strenuous effort to get back on top of the wardrobe. I was agile as a little monkey after a while. My brother enjoyed these nightly scenes and it was probably then that he decided to specialize in forensic psychiatry. His favorite books at this time were on forensic medicine and pathology. He was as happy in his world as I was in mine.

When the babysitter came over and tried to watch TV or talk on the phone, I brought my mattress downstairs and covered it with cushions and bedspreads. Then I climbed the stairs, ran the length of the upstairs landing, and soared over the banister to the makeshift landing pad. This was quite impressive, I felt, but noisy since I screeched "Banzai!" or imitated the scream of a Stuka dive bomber in a precipitous descent. She would come out, look at the mattress and me, say "Jesus" and go back to the TV or the phone. She never liked babysitting me because I never spoke and only stared at her or else flew over the banister. I have to admit I would have found it unsettling too, and I don't get perplexed easily. The line of least resistance suited the babysitter fine. And me. She never seemed worried that I might injure myself or else she hoped for it.

My father died when I was young and my mother married again. While he was alive he used to say to my mother "That guy is a fecking genius, Missus."

My mother wasn't convinced. I once heard them arguing.

"That kid is a fucking psycho. Where did we get him?"

"He's an angel, really," my father replied in a quiet tone.

"A fallen angel, more like. He leaps off the wardrobe, you know. I can never catch him but the mattress has a big depression in it."

"Emm... maybe," my father replied.

It reminded me of the Emo Philip's joke about overhearing his parents argue... "I told you he would live," the mother complains. It wasn't that bad, but it was bad enough.

I tried to curtail my flights so my father would not have

to defend me as much. He was gentle and bright and introverted. When he died from a massive brain hemorrhage, I think his body decided to self-implode because he did not fit easily into this world.

I used to watch him leave for work before dawn from my perch on the windowsill of our bedroom. He made preparations for his journey in the yard. Sometimes he glanced up to the window as if he sensed I was there and I eased back into shadow. He'd take out the bicycle, close the front door, triple-check to see if it was closed, hang his lunch bag from the handlebars and put on bicycle clips which he kept on the crossbar. Then in one quick movement, holding the bike steady, his left foot on the pedal, he pushed the bike into precarious tilted motion until he brought his other leg over the crossbar to correct the imbalance. The symmetry and locomotion of it all reminded me of a plane taxiing down a temporary airstrip built close to a war front. I could hear the whir of the dynamo fading as he cycled down the street.

I stayed there for a while on the narrow window ledge shivering in the darkness in case he had forgotten anything. Sometimes he re-entered the house before he left. When I heard him coming up the stairs I jumped into bed and pretended I was asleep. He would stand at the door for a few minutes or come in and put his hand to my throat to check that I was breathing. I could smell the bicycle oil on his hands and he left a frosty patina on my throat.

The night he died I re-launched my unconventional and uncompromising flights with renewed vigor. It was like the bombing of Dresden. I was on all night sorties until I finally fell exhausted. My brother watched me with concern. When I finally landed for the last time, he put down his book, *Dissection for Beginners*, and cradled me in his arms and I cried until I fell asleep.

Drive This

My mother started taking driving lessons after my father died. I didn't mean to kill him so early. Accidents do happen, you know. But he had it coming.

It's hard enough for teenagers to listen to pompous instructors droning on about dual control, parallel parking, road etiquette and emergency breaking, but for a mature adult it's grating. Not to mention the body odors and fatuous comments you have to shield. You also have to tolerate being spoken to like your brain is a blocked carburetor. For someone of my mother's age, it's more difficult to acquire new motor skills, especially since her sense of direction was askew in the first place.

She was a district nurse in Galway and cycled through the grim gray streets visiting the house-bound sick in the tough City Council estates which we called hell—I mean home. The skinheads who lounged at street corners with their dogs and skinhead girls were respectful toward my mother and allowed her safe passage because one day they might need her. For their parents and grandparents, she drained suppurating wounds, removed stitches, gave bed baths and hurt her back lifting heavy immobile bastards (as she called them) to change dressings.

She cycled through the black evenings and the icy wind and rain flying in off the Atlantic chaffed her hands and face. When she got home she could barely move her hands. They were red and blotchy and icy to the touch.

"Ma—I'll make you some tea."

21

She sat at the kitchen table with the hot sweet tea in her hands and nodded at me in thanks.

She began the driving lessons to get away from the wind and rain. And to supplement the lost income of my father. She thought she would also be safer from the skinheads' Alsatians. Those dogs were more labile than their owners and watched her approach in the pale evening light with total concentration. She felt they might one day slip free from the long chain leashes the pale skinheads used to tether them and tear her and her bicycle to pieces.

❧

I once was savaged by an Alsatian, so she was right to be cautious. It was Sunday morning. I was doing God's work—collecting envelopes from the neighbors with donations for the church—and when I jumped the separating wall of a neighbor's garden, Nelson spotted me and began chomping. I stuck a knife in the wall of his heart so it slowed him down a bit. But he did damage. My father jumped the wall and hit him with a shovel that split his head open. Luckily, Nelson let me go at that stage. I retrieved the knife and forgot about the church envelope. Obviously, God was having a good laugh. Enough about me.

❧

She enrolled in 'The Excellent Driver School of Motoring,' but the only excellent thing about it was the income the driving instructor made. He lived in the comfortable west side of Galway City, far far away from the hard streets that bred skinheads and delinquents of all hues. His instructions were curt and vague and haphazard. He admonished my mother over every minor error. He had a fixation about emergency stops and when she failed to effect these to his satisfaction, he complained ad nauseam. He kept returning to emergency stops even though they are rarely in the driving test. Besides, the only emergency stop worth doing is ramming the fucking brakes through the floor and hoping for the best.

22

My mother came home from these lessons chastised and dispirited. Sometimes she cried when she got inside the door. I had never seen that before. I told her to quit the lessons. I told her I would kill Mr. Excellent Driver School or at least get her skinhead admirers from Shantalla and the Claddagh and Bohermore to do it. But she declined my generous offer, laughing, and said I'll take that tea instead. Every Tuesday she went to those lessons with grim determination and dread and courage.

After twelve weeks, she had her test and passed. I thought it was divine intervention. The night after, we celebrated with two cups of tea instead of one. I left the house and headed to the lonesome west of Salthill, where the instructor lived. I waited in the shadow of the bushes of his front garden. When he drove into the driveway and got out of the car, I walked up silently behind him and hit him on the back of the head with a sock full of stones. He collapsed like a bullock felled with a bolt-gun. I retrieved the can of petrol from the trunk of his car. Rule Number Five of the Excellent Driver Code: "Every Excellent Driver should carry a spare gallon of fuel." He would be sorry he came up with that one. I doused the car all over inside and out and threw a match in.

The flames whooshed into the dark Galway sky with blue orange rapture. Or was that me?

"Try an emergency stop now," I said.

As I walked away, I felt the heat at my back. It felt good.

I suppose I went a bit overboard. Sometimes I'm impulsive. Dumping the driving instructor into the open trunk at the last minute before throwing the match in is probably one example.

He had it coming, though.

Just like daddy.

The Butterfly Love Song

When the doorbell rang, I was in the TV room. We rarely had visitors. My mother didn't even like us coming home from school, so casual callers were infrequent and unwelcome. I was usually forced to crawl on my belly to the front door, like a child commando, to decipher who was outside. I incorporated forward rolls and somersaults to keep it interesting. The upper part of the door was beveled glass. Because of the distortion, it could have been a Martian or Marilyn Monroe or Mrs. Molloy from down the street (the least favored option). She was so house-proud. Our house was like a tenement in comparison. Plus, it was a tenement. I relayed back to my mother, as she loitered in the kitchen doorway with a Sweet Afton in her hand and an anxious look, my best estimate of the enemy. If I guessed wrong I would be in trouble, so usually I said "It's the tinkers." Like body counts in Vietnam, it was mythical.

She'd say "Fucking knackers, they can go and shite!"

She had a way with words.

I liked the tinkers myself. They rode bareback through our concrete streets clutching the ragged manes of their piebald ponies, the metal of the horse shoes echoing in the valley of high-rise flats, a high-fidelity warrior sound on a lost trail. They rode their horses with majestic indifference and disdain. That's how I wanted to negotiate my way through my teens. It didn't work. See below.

The local parish priest was the only one that managed to breach the citadel of our council flat on a regular basis. He would bend down, push back the letter slot and shout—

"Missus? It's me. Father Barry."

He was the father of a chubby red-haired baby boy in the next parish. He had a car. He could travel. Travel broadens the mind. I would shout back, "Ma, it's Father-father." I imagined the baby was christened Barry. Hence Barry Barry. Hence the wee baby bastard Barry Barry. I was a bit of a wordsmith. He wouldn't survive the schoolyard long with an appellation like that. I barely survived myself.

My mother didn't like this irreverence to Father Barry, but she wouldn't retaliate while I was prone on the floor looking up at the blinking eyes of father Barry through the letter slot. Father Barry could do no wrong, as far as my mother was concerned. Even if Father Barry was a daddy.

"Bless you, my son," Father Barry would say, patting me on the head as he brushed past on his way to the kitchen. It was a bit ambiguous but I tried not to think about it. The last thing I needed was a little red-haired half-brother bastard in the adjoining parish. Talk about a liability.

It would be impossible for me to evoke any semblance of sang-froid in such circumstances. I was taking French at school so I could join the Foreign Legion, lose my identity, lay down withering fields of fire and return a hero to impress les filles. Anyway, at our house I think Father Barry was only interested in parochial matters like collecting the weekly money for the building of Mervue Community Center where teenagers would gather in the years to come to make babies in the dark alley behind. No travel involved.

My mother learned Morse code while she was training to be a nurse in Gloucester after the war, so she instructed us how to tap on the door with the codes: "THIS IS VICTOR" or "THIS IS ROB." She would wait until the full sentence was tapped out before letting you in. This was hard when the wind and rain and sleet were chaffing the exposed skin of your legs. I found a book in the library on Morse code so I started embellishing. "THIS IS YOUR ONLY BEGOTTEN

SON" or "THIS IS BARRY BARRY THE FATHER'S SON" or "THIS IS THE MILKMAN" or "THIS IS NOT A LOVE SONG" or "DIS IS A GALL-WAY AKCENT."

"Very fucking funny," she would say when she eventually let me in. After a while, she would swing the door open as soon as I got to "THIS" so the fun went out of it. I can still use Morse code if the need arises.

When we started attending secondary school, she gave us house keys. They were tied around our necks, attached to our scapulars. She could think of nowhere safer. It was tricky because as you put the key in the door she was likely to pull it open quickly, pulling you inwards, the scapulars cutting into your neck, you stumbling over the threshold. When you removed the key from around your neck before opening the door she never yanked it open.

She also decided to end our isolationist policy. Glasnost was in effect. If the Russians could do it, so could she. She was an avid news junkie. Now she wanted the door answered immediately in case we'd miss anything. It was a bit late. Because of years of unanswered bells, no neighbors called anymore.

&

The Leepers lived above us. Mister Leeper was a master butcher. One of his daughters wore a white glove. It was rumored to cover a hand withered since birth. We preferred to think that Mister Leeper had loped it off by mistake while practicing arcane rasher-cutting rituals. I wanted to shake hands with her to see how it felt. I shook hands with everyone I met, so it was a plausible approach. I was kind of a throwback to the previous century. She managed to avoid all contact with me, so the wish went unfilled. Perhaps like her glove.

I sang: Jeepers creepers, what's de fuckin' story with dem Leepers?

I was a bit of a balladeer.

Laura Leeper increased my interest in morbid anatomy.

26

My brother Rob already had books on anatomy from the college library (purloined) and Peddler Bookshop (shoplifted). Medical students from the university sold them after they graduated and went off to Africa for a few months to practice dubious surgical procedures on the locals, who would not complain, before they swept back to Galway to set up practice in the Crescent where the smell of money was muted only by the sweet smell of lilacs in the cultivated gardens of the elegant Victorian townhouses.

The Peddler was owned by the first openly gay teenager from the local housing estate. He wasn't killed, which was a miracle. He was handsome and amusing, but I saw his distressed look in the Warwick Hotel where he fumbled and stumbled around the periphery of the dance-floor as two hundred heterosexual teenagers vied for the attention of the opposite sex while he wandered smitten and forlorn.

❧

The Lambs lived on one side of us. They were quiet. The Rabbits lived on the other side. They were not. All the boys ended up in jail. They picked magic mushrooms on damp summer mornings on the racecourse a few miles away to get a head start even though they didn't need it. They were hardwired for delinquency. All the sisters went to college and married engineers and doctors, so were able to afford bail money and lawyers for all the incarcerated Rabbit boys. I was studying Mendel in my spare time, so was fascinated by this glaring dichotomy between the Rabbit boys and the Rabbit girls. The Rabbit boys were twitchy, never still, never silent, never at ease, never safe. The Rabbit girls were subtle, savvy, silent, social, sartorial. Mendel would have abandoned the pea plant experiments if he lived next door to the Rabbits.

I liked the Lambs because the name reminded me of holidays on my grandmother's farm in Mayo. Every Friday the red truck stopped at the bottom of the rough driveway and I would race down to peer into the hatch of the travelling shop while the owner (and driver) took up his post and peered back at me. My grandmother bought pan loaves, grain for the chickens, salt, tea, sugar (all weighed by the driver and packaged in small brown bags), plug tobacco for my grandfather and a pot of Lamb's jam. Nothing tasted better. That's why I liked the Lambs living beside us. Also, they weren't the Rabbits.

Sara Joyce lived downstairs. She was almost deaf and so had the TV and radio switched to maximum volume. We didn't need to switch our radio on if we didn't want to. You could hear about the latest factory closures through the floor. Her skin was black from years of sitting in front of open hearths with the turf smoke tattooing black molecular smuts into her epidermis. She was from the same village as my mother and pined after it so she cried whenever they met on the stairwell. That's another reason my mother haunted our rooms, avoiding Sara Joyce and her own childhood traumas, all the while sizing me up, troubled, sozzled. It was interesting to hear TV programs blaring from Sara's flat while our own TV was on. It produced a remarkable stereophonic effect with floor vibrations. After a while you got used to it. After a while you can get used to anything.

❧

"Get that, will ya?" my mother shouted from the kitchen.

I ignored her. Sometimes she forgot, especially if it was just one ring and she was drinking. Anyway my favorite program was on, an hour-long nature documentary on tropical predators.

After a few seconds when the bell rang again she walked to the doorway and, pointing at me and then the door, said "Answer that fucking door or I'll put you through it."

Fair enough. Beveled glass could ruin your complexion. She was dangerous when she was drunk.

"Stop wearing that outfit," she said. "It gets on my nerves. If you want to live in the Amazon basin why don't you just fuck off there with yourself."

I was only thirteen, so thought it was a bit harsh. She could cut you with words like a blade through a baby bunny. That is, the whole way through.

I wished I did live in the Amazon basin. I was wearing a dashing safari outfit I bought at the Vincent de Paul thrift shop on Sea Road. It was a bit big, but did the trick. I wore it when I was watching nature and wildlife specials. The bell rang again.

She looked at the door and back at me.

I got up from the TV. In the hallway there was a black and white photograph of my mother. It was a school outing etched for the last forty years in a Farrell's Friendly Family Foto. She wore a school uniform and a straw boater. When she wasn't around I took it down and held it close to my eyes, the glass distorting the image, trying to decipher the meaning of what she had been. Once she was just a girl. She sat on the banks of a stream with her long sallow legs dipped into the rushing water, a bright open smile, now trapped in a frown by a snare of drink and depression. I wanted to go back in time and watch her passing the road, to see that smile I never saw. I'm a bit of a hopeless romantic, I suppose.

The bell was ringing without cease now. I trudged to the door.

When I opened it, I knew. Knew I shouldn't. Knew it was trouble, double trouble. The Block twins. They scanned me with their blue-black eyes, deep-sea-and-no-way-back-from-full-fathom-five eyes, lost eyes, do-something-man and we'll pluck out your eyes, eyes.

Block A inspected me while he kept his finger on the buzzer.

"I'm here," I said.

He held it depressed a moment longer.

I felt like closing the door. Actually I felt like smashing it shut and nailing it up. I felt like puking. They instilled complete motor-neuron-function dysfunction once you were in range of them. They were lean and elegant and as steely as flick knives. They were sleek with venom and bravery and fighting power. They fought in silence, balletic-street-fighting kings, sculpting blows and kicks into a fierce pugilistic embrace, laying foes down on wet macadam, kissing with elbows and knuckles and knees and steel toe caps.

Anyway, I was petrified. I felt like severing those high-beam-light eyes out of their sockets so I wouldn't have to see them anymore. I felt like piercing their hearts with steel-tipped arrows. I had a crossbow in my room. I carried it around when *Robin Hood* was on TV, but it might as well have been buried under the sea. It was très beaucoup malade, I can tell you.

Block A stuck his boot in the doorframe. At least it wasn't my face. I looked down at the high-polished boots. Block B leaned nonchalantly against the wall of the house, blowing cigarette smoke into the cool black night. With languorous rhythm and great skill he flicked, opened and closed a butterfly knife. The moon glinted off its blade in high lustrous tints.

Block A, "Doctor Fuckingeejitston, I presume." He laughed. I looked down at my safari outfit. At least he was au fait with the old African history and exploration stuff.

Block A, "What the fucking fuck is that?"

He pulled the butterfly net out of my hand. It burned my skin as he jerked it free. I used it as a prop with the safari ensemble. It was the nearest equivalent to a naturalist's insect net I could find. I forgot I was carrying it when I answered the door.

He looked at me like a pit-bull views a supine baby before tearing it asunder. He showed it to Block B. Block A mimicked kung fu fighting stances, making exaggerated ahh-soo sounds. Block B looked on impassively, just kept flicking his knife in the pale moonlight. Dancing in the moonlight. On that long hot summer night. Block A then broke the flimsy bamboo pole of the net over his knee. It sounded like breaking a baby's back. He threw the pieces away into the darkness. "You'll be next," he said to me. I believed him.

Block A, "My sister wants you to come over tomorrow night."

It could have been worse. I suppose.

"What! You sure you have the right guy?"

"Yeah, we don't believe it either, but that's it. You're it."

"I'm not sure I can, actually."

"Actually, fuck you. Actually you're her date until she says different, actually."

I would try to remember not to say actually again.

"I don't get it."

"What don't you get?"

"I don't know. I just don't get it. I barely know her."

"Well, you will soon. Call around tomorrow night at seven. If you don't, you'll get it."

I knew what that meant. The other it. The blue-black, blood-bruised, deep-tissue, kicked to bits it.

Block A pushed me back against the wall. It had a pebble-dash effect with nodules of lumpy concrete icing. My head hit the wall with enough force for blood to run from the back of my scalp. I could feel it seeping down the back of my neck past the collar of my safari jacket.

He removed his boot from the doorway.

"Okay safari-head. Tomorrow at the house. Don't wear that gear."

Even I knew this.

When they got to the gate they looked back. They blew me kisses.

My mother came to the door.

"What do the Blockheads want?"

I was in an agitated state.

"Their sister wants me to call around tomorrow night."

"So what? No need to have a meltdown. She's just a girl."

I moved past her. The smell of drink shrouded me.

"Don't wear that outfit, though," she called at my back.

"Jesus Christ! I know, I know."

Did everyone think I was thick?

I tried to calm myself.

Okay. Just a girl just a girl just a girl.

She wasn't.

Lucy Block was a warrior with pearl-gray eyes. Malevolence cubed. She shone like a beacon in this sea of concrete and decay. She shone like a beacon until you sailed too close. Then you knew a hundred miles was too close. Ship aground, all hands lost. Caustic, fourteen, filigreed-defiance, a pagan life-force shone off her. A rocker, king of the girls, smoker, brawler, sullen, muted, raging. Just my type. Definitely not.

In the school corridor I watched for her shaved head bobbing among the sea of students. She ignored me. Her coterie were chips off the old bollocks: Martin Savage, John 'Basher' Barret, Sean Laffey (he never laughed), Jo 'Killer' Killkelly. You get the picture. I was no way in the picture. Not even a random dust mote in the negative.

I thought it was a trap or else that she liked me. Fuck. I avoided direct contact with girls. I don't know where boys are from, but girls are from Cubist, a planet out of my constellation. Girls scope out the skies of emotion and elegance on elliptical orbits that I can't track. I had more of a chance of joining the Legion at thirteen as I had of negotiating the mental and social culverts of a date with Lucy Block.

My teenage aunt said I was pale and interesting. I avoided the sun. She practiced dancing with me before she went out on Friday nights to trawl for an eligible skinhead at the local dancing emporium, The Snake. I am not joking. So I could dance if I was stuck to impress. I practiced the pogo for hours in front of the mirror. I liked the pogo the best. I could dance it all night if I had to. I felt like a Maasai warrior as I practiced in my bedroom. I had great calf muscles after a few months. My mother would hammer on the ceiling.

"Quit that fucking racket."

She gave up in the end.

"That fucker is nuts," she said to her sister, my dancing

partner aunt. My aunt blew smoke at the ceiling.

"Nah, he's fine."

While cleaning the blood from the collar of my safari jacket, I missed half the lifecycle of the python on TV. Outside, the dark night shimmered with Blades on street corners. My broken net lay on the wet concrete, hidden in the dark, forgotten. Butterfly knifes sang love songs. Lucy Block waited.

✤

I didn't sleep all night. I saw her in the school corridor the next day. She looked right through me as usual. I saw the Block twins and ducked into an open doorway. They stopped outside the classroom and looked in. I had to pretend I was just leaving and nodded at them as I left.

"Tarzan, don't forget about tonight," they shouted after me.

"Very droll," I said. To myself. And kept walking.

Rumor had spread that the Block twins called the night before. Since I was still walking, my prestige grew among my schoolmates but I could not savor it.

"What did they want?"

"Nothing."

"How come you're alive?"

"I don't know."

"Do you have internal injuries that we can't see?"

"Yes."

I kept saying.

It's only a girl.

It's only a girl.

It's only a girl.

It's only the Black Death.

Same reassuring effect.

At 6:59 in the evening (fashionably early) I called around to chez Block. Thank God the twins were out. Block mere answered the door and she did a double take. Not a Blade carrying the same, just me, the suitor in shining armor with a tenuous grasp of French, sexuality, fashion, reality. She turned around and shouted, "It's the butterfly nut."

I couldn't believe the Blocks told their mother. I imagined they passed each other in sullen silence in the hallways and narrow corridors of the house. Was nothing sacred?

"You better come in, I suppose."

She herded me through the hallway into the TV room. I use the term loosely. Lucy was sitting on the sofa watching TV. She slowly looked up at me. I gave her a hesitant half-salute.

"What do you want?"

"I thought I was supposed to call around."

"Did you?"

"Actually, I thought it was all arranged."

I was holding my own so far. Well, not really.

"Actually, take it easy. Your sense of humor is zero. Can't you see I'm all dressed up?"

I saw straight away.

"Would you like tea before we cause the sensation of the year?"

"Ah, no. I just cleaned my teeth."

Jesus, what an answer.

"Ah, I will probably spill it on myself," I added.

Even worse.

Or on the black Alsatian who was sniffing my crotch while I stood at the door.

"Killer, sit down," called the mother.

I felt much safer. Killer! Jaysus!

"I'll make it anyway," Lucy said. "Sit down. Killer, stay."

I sat on the sofa while the mother watched me. Joan Jet played on the TV. Both were fascinating. Joan Jet was safer. Killer sat watching the TV and kept turning his head to look back at me.

"You're not one of the usual fuckers who come to see her."

I studied Joan Jet's image intently, as if I didn't hear the mother.

"No, ma'am," I said eventually, since I could feel her eyes on me.

"No ma'am. Christ, what century are you from?"

I wasn't sure of that myself.

Lucy came back with the tea. I tried to manage it without spilling any.

"Back soon," she said and went upstairs.

"Where are the twins?" I ventured after a while to the mother.

"The Blockheads are out."

Okay, that didn't get far. I just sat there drinking the tea and trying to not sweat too much.

When Lucy came down, she said "let's go."

I jumped to attention and the cup went flying. The mother jerked back as if I had detonated an artillery shell. Killer leapt up and went for me. I did one of my pogo jumps and the dog passed safely below.

Both mother and daughter looked up at me in obvious admiration as I flew ceiling-ward. I was impressed myself. Things were looking up.

Killer careened into the television and it quieted him before he had a chance to make a second attempt at me. The TV toppled in slow motion. Before anyone could grab it, it fell from its precarious stand onto the floor. Sparks flew, but not between myself and Lucy Block. They flew from the back of the set with an intensity that surprised me. Like the back-fire from a Katyusha rocket. The lights in the room flickered once, then died. Killer started growling. The mother started cursing and flicked her cigarette lighter on. I saw her trip over Killer as she tried to escape into the kitchen. The lighter flying through the air and the flame purged.

I waited in the dark with the cigarette smoke spoiling my white skin and pink lungs, my radar sounding Lucy Block, my hands sweating, my calves tingling, my life flashing in front of me—the Blockheads feeding me to Killer, my mother sighing over my open grave, the mourners doing the pogo, my aunt weeping into the bony shoulder of her boyfriend's bomber jacket.

Well, things can't get any worse, I thought.

But I was wrong.

Night at the Banshee

We got to the Banshee around six and parked out front. Rowley territory, so we didn't have a problem. No tickets. No fines. No cops. It's owned by my uncle Gerry Rowley, which rhymes with growly, which he could be but usually wasn't especially around family. The Banshee is on Dorchester Avenue in South Boston. It's a pub and restaurant. It's an Irish story. It's a grand story.

Uncle Gerry's manager Frank came over to us and smiled at my cousin.

"Hi, Susan. Good to see you. Your father is in back. He's in a meeting but won't be too long."

"That's fine—don't interrupt him. We've come to have our tea!"

"That's grand. We're honored of course."

He looked like he was flirting with her and I could see they liked each other. I adopted my sullen look and didn't say anything when I shook hands with him as she introduced us.

"This is my cousin from Ireland. Isn't he handsome?"

"He certainly is."

"But I saw him first."

"Okay, so!"

They laughed.

So he was gay. Okay. Panic over. I would let him live. I adopted my un-sullen look.

"Nice to meet you," I said.

I can be fickle.

We sat at a table near the front. Susan waved to people

at different tables. Various college types. I just nodded sagely as if I knew what it was all about. My social interaction skills were not the best. My unorthodox upbringing had warped them forever. I was sixteen but didn't look or feel it.

Susan got up and went off to talk to some of her friends.

Frank asked "How old are you anyway? You look about twelve."

"I'm a vegetarian."

"How does that help?"

"It keeps you young looking. You should try it."

"Good one. You sure have a smart mouth."

"I can't help being smart."

"See what I mean?"

Susan came back and sat down and sighed contentedly and grabbed the menu from me.

"I don't know why I'm so popular."

"Yeah it's hard to figure, okay."

She punched me on the shoulder. A pretty good one. I picked up another menu and looked at the offering, but it was carnivore heaven.

When the waiter came I said "Chips, beans and rice, and a pot of tea."

Susan laughed and Frank smirked.

I tensed, but Susan touched my arm and said "I'll have the same." Frank laughed and I smiled, and that was that. No problem.

"You should try it, Frank. It's good for you," Susan said.

He hesitated. The daughter of the boss, or his carnivorous hardwiring? The brain won, no problem.

"No, Susan. I'll stick with the meat. That vegetarian stuff would kill me at this stage."

"Okay, but don't expect us to visit you in the cancer ward," Susan said.

"I'll take my chances. It'll take more than one more steak to land me in hospital."

He was right.

"I'll have the steak. Rare as you can make it, garsoon," he said to the waiter.

"Chips are French fries in case you don't know," Susan said to the waiter as he left with the order.

I'd say he knew already. This was Southie, after all.

I looked around. The place was full. Irish, Irish-Americans. First, second and third generation Irish. Waiters and bar-staff rushed to fill orders and waitresses tried to avoid chat-up lines they heard before. A relaxed atmosphere, but I was certain no one walked away without paying. There was noise from the kitchens and from the cutlery hitting tables and from the tills chiming, but the place was spacious and bright and airy. There were booths and plenty of big tables that could seat a generous number of customers, not like those McDonalds cesspools where your arse wants to slip off the curved seats after five minutes, which is what they want. Turnover, in more ways than one.

Uncle Gerry joined us. He gave Susan a kiss and looked at me.

"How's Billy the Kid?" he asked, laughing. He must have heard about my penchant for guns from home, I suppose. My mother was a blabbermouth. Unlike my votre self.

"I'm not a kid," I said, and managed a wan smile.

"Look, Frank," Gerry said. "A smile. We're making progress."

Frank looked over, but missed my thin smile.

He didn't miss the bullets though.

He was hit in the shoulder twice. I saw two crimson rosettes appear, followed by the immense noise of several handguns. I looked up. There were three skinny white guys firing at us. All three had two handguns each, a real Wild West scene. The waiter behind us fell—two shots to the head, no chance. Beer, change, the tray and his Irish blood went flying. A waitress, barman and two customers at the table directly behind us also fell injured. They were firing wild and high. They must have been nervous. Uncle Gerry was hit in the head, blood cascading from his ears. Bad. Messy.

Susan was screaming along with most of the customers and staff. Frank had risen as soon as the shooting started and, even though he was hit twice, he flung a plate of bread rolls reflexively and tried to pull his pistol. However, he fell and hit the table before falling to the floor, pulling the table-cloth and the cutlery with him.

I jumped in front of Susan to shield her from any bullets. I am a throwback to a previous age of chivalry. My mother drilled it into us. It's an automatic action now. I have to stand up if introduced to a female. I have to stand up for females. Everyone has fatal flaws. One bullet grazed my temple and another grazed my shoulder and that was the end of that Aran sweater. The pain was immense. I sat on my arse on the floor with an upturned table in front of me. With Susan behind me, I scuttled back as far as I could. She hadn't stopped screaming and neither had anyone else, but I didn't care about them. I grabbed Frank's pistol from his holster and waited, crouched.

I heard all six guns dry-fire and jumped up from the overturned table and shot the first guy nearest me in the cheek. He was just reloading. He shouldn't have used a .22 from so far away. It's great for executions up close, but useless over three feet. The side of his head exploded. The second guy looked up and I shot him above the left eyebrow. Miracle shot. He lost his brain and his life. The third guy was loaded and started firing at me. I stood and kept walking toward him, firing as I went. It was like a slow motion clip from a gangster film or Wyatt Earp in a saloon shoot-out. I felt brilliant and invincible. I was totally alive. I knew he couldn't hit me. I kept walking. I even smiled.

He faltered and ran and slipped on blood and spilt beer, but got to his feet again and ran. I ran after him. Susan was calling me. Sirens were approaching. He tripped near the door. I was beside him in a moment.

"Drop the gun."

He did.

"Open your mouth."

He did.

I jammed it in.

"Say goodbye."

He did (surprisingly).

I shot his head and baseball cap off.

I noticed he was wearing a small silver swastika charm around his neck.

Charming.

I ran back to Frank and grabbed him by the collar.

"You call yourself a fucking bodyguard?" I pressed the pistol against his head. "I ought to blow your brains out."

Instead, I pointed the gun at my temple and fired. I knew it was out of shells. I counted during the gunfight. They flinched. They looked impressed. I was impressed myself.

Infected

I was the youngest Aryan Youth in Galway, or Ireland, or the world probably, when I joined the National Socialist Workers' Party of Great Britain and Ireland (NSWPGBI). Even the Third Reich had a minimum entry age of thirteen, but I was always an innovator. I was twelve. Membership numbers in Ireland were too few to enroll in person, so my induction papers arrived by post. I knew what they were because of an embossed eagle on the back of the envelope. I swore allegiance to the party, to Aryan ideals, pure blood, perfection.

The envelope included an armband with an SS lightning bolt which I wore day and night. As I marched back and forth in my bedroom, I admired the armband and my Aryan profile in the wardrobe mirror. I had the best goose-step in Galway. I developed amazing thigh and calf muscles. My mother would knock on the ceiling.

"What the fuck is going on up there?" she would shout. "That guy is a psycho," she would say to my father.

He didn't respond. He just kept polishing and repairing my shoes as I wore out the leather.

I felt I had the right credentials for leading the life of an aesthete demanded by the party and an inherent dedication to the party's objectives. The aim of seducing Aryan maidens would be a problem since I was pathologically shy. When asked at family weddings or birthdays to dance with girls, I refused and blushed. I turned and then goose-stepped away. That would show them.

I read the speeches of Adolf Hitler and his deputy, Rudolph Hess, whose Germanic bearing and deep-seated eyes attracted me. I wrote to Hess in Spandau prison in East Berlin but the letters always came back "Return to sender— Not at this address." In fact, he was the only person at that address.

I liked the work of the Nazi architect Albert Speer who designed the spectacles of Nuremburg—massed troops in symmetric phalanges, flags and banners in the millions recalling the legions of Rome, eagles, swastikas, high beam arc lights streaming into the skies, and the hundred foot high columns of the Nuremburg arena.

At night, I tuned our radio to long wave in order to pick up a German station and played it while I marched. I found a copy of an LP in a charity shop that had "Deutschland über Alles" as a track, so I played that until the grooves in the vinyl wore out. I was worn out myself from marching.

I was the first child in Galway (or again the world probably) who requested the speeches of Hitler in their original German from the British Library through interlibrary loan. The staff in the Galway Public Library in Court House Square didn't know how to request an ILL, so I was sent to the university library where the college librarian, although taken aback, authorized the request in the interests of academic freedom and scholarship. When a postcard arrived to the house, my mother said "What the hell is an ILL?" I tried to explain, but after thirty seconds she walked away and went outside and lit another Sweet Afton.

I memorized Hitler's speeches in German, but I had no idea what I was saying, so I had to get the translations— again through ILL. By now the staff in the university library knew me. They mimicked the Seig Heil salute when the librarian was not there, and naturally I would return it. The floor was polished teak, so the metal cleats in my shoes made a satisfying noise when I struck the floor to complete the full salute. I was really tempted to march across the long floor so I could demonstrate my perfect goose-stepping, but I restrained myself.

I mimicked Hitler's tepid salutes, the facial grimaces. I wasn't keen on the haircut and lacked facial hair so the moustache was a nonstarter. I preferred Rudolf Hess's clean cut classical Germanic features anyway.

To keep my options open, however, I did consult with Chick, the local barber, to see if he could cut my hair like Hitler—I brought a volume of *Encyclopedia Brittanica* to show him. It was very heavy, and by the time I reached Dominick Street I was faltering.

"I know how he had his hair," he said. "It's a disgrace. That Eva Braun one must have been clinically blind."

Chick didn't drink or smoke, but he knocked guys out on the dance floor of the Hanger and Seapoint. He kept wild ponies in his council estate garden and held impromptu races on hot summer afternoons.

"If you want your hair cut like one of our 1916 martyrs, I can do that. They had great heads of Irish hair before the British murderers blew their heads off with volleys of rifle bullets in Kilmainhaim jail." (I didn't want to tell him they were shot in the heart—he had a thing about heads.)

I should not have asked about Hitler's hair while he was cutting mine. He lost his concentration and want on automatic pilot so when he emerged from his reverie, I was the first skinhead in Ireland in addition to being the youngest Aryan Youth recruit. I suppose it was fitting.

My mother hit me when I walked in.

"What kind of a fucking haircut is that? Wait until your father gets home. Get up those stairs."

And then my father came home.

"Great hair cut," he said. "You look like an Apache."

"Apache's have long hair."

I was a stickler for detail.

"Do they? Well, a Kiowa or a Comanche so?"

"No, the closest would be a Mohican."

"Okay, you look like a Mohican—don't do it again. Your mother will scalp both of us."

He laughed at that.

I didn't. I had no sense of humor. I'm a bit better now.

I didn't care. With my shaved head, I could pretend I was an SS guard. I thought it all fit. I was in love with Stuka dive bombers, Blitzkrieg, Unterseeboots, Messerschmidts, and Panzers.

While other teenagers were drawing romantic hearts pierced with arrows, I was drawing swastikas or the intertwined oak leaf clusters awarded for bravery to Stuka pilots. I had a thing about Stukas. I drew Iron Crosses and the lighting bolt SS insignia. I sure was one committed little Nazi neophyte.

Ireland had strong links with Germany, which helped mold my benign outlook. Germany was the natural ally of the IRA because any enemy of England was a friend of Ireland. Germany provided the IRA with weapons. They dropped off IRA men from submarines off the Irish coast. The most common handgun used by the IRA was the Luger.

We were neutral in World War II to show Britain that we were indeed independent after eight hundred years of subjugation. This is why President de Valera signed the book of condolences at the German Embassy in Dublin after Hitler did everyone a favor.

Hitler had an Irish nephew named William who settled in Berlin when World War II broke out and dressed like his famous uncle—even crossing his arms and wearing the same type of mustache. It appeared megalomania ran in the family, although in William's case it was more benign. Hitler hated his 'dreadful nephew' and had no family allegiance of any kind. He said he did not become Chancellor to give jobs to relatives. Irish politicians, take note. He was serious because when the village in Austria unveiled a plaque to commemorate his birth place, he ordered the town to be used as an artillery range. All his relatives in the graveyard were blown to smithereens as a result.

William could have played soccer for Ireland, but would need a thick skin—not a noted feature of Hitler family.

"Hitler, ya blind bollicks. Shoot for the fooken goal."

"Hitler, ya dumkoff. Blitzkrieg the fooken goal mouth why don't ya?"

We are hard to please. We all knew dumkoff from reading the *Victor* comic. "Donner und Blitzen" was another catchy phrase we assimilated.

I taped the sound of the air raid siren at the local fire station on Father Griffin Road and played it back when I lay in bed shining the light into the clusters of Stuka models suspended in the darkness. It took a long time to accumulate a decent recording because the siren only sounded when there was a major fire. So there was a lot of sitting around at the feet of the statue of Father Griffin for the next fire and the next installment of the siren symphony.

Although on paper and in my mind I had good credentials for the membership of the NSWPGBI, I ran into problems. The party leader in Dublin was stabbed, which lessened my enthusiasm. They wanted to re-reunite Ireland with England. That was a non-starter since all my relatives were ex-IRA members who still carried well-oiled revolvers and knew how to use them. I decided to resign. I liked to follow protocol, so I wrote back to HQ in Dublin to give them the bad news. I did not want to be executed by one of my own relatives. An Irish pastime. Also, I seemed to be the only member in Galway. And since I was twelve, I found it hard to hunt down 'undesirables'.

One such group in Galway that I could identify were lithe Chinese waiters who chain-smoked thin cigarettes and practiced complex kung fu katas with fluid grace in the back yard of the Golden Palace on Mainguard Street. Since they fed half of Galway, I knew I could not touch them. Anyway, I was no match for their disabling roundhouse kicks. Anyway, they weren't in the leaflets. Anyway, I loved Bruce Lee.

The only black people in Galway were the Cazabons from Philadelphia who moved with supple, sleek movements through the corridors of our school, who played basketball with finesse and skill, who would kill me if I started anything. I liked how they talked and walked and played electric guitar and looked at girls with languorous delight. They could probably make more headway with the Aryan maidens than I ever would.

One day I was in the Peddler Bookshop in Middle Street where I kept a close watch on the Chinese restaurant across the road and also hid from the marauding Rattlesnakes. They did not even know what Nazis were. I was a bit uncomfortable in the Peddler because the owner was a member of another minority group I was supposed to be wiping out. He was the first gay guy from the concrete bunkers of Mervue. Like the Chinese and the Cazabons, I was giving him leeway as well. He had a great shop, so I let it slide. I was faltering on all fronts. In the Peddler, I moved away from the windows to the back section in the unlikely event that the Rattlesnakes would look in. They had as much regard for books as the Nazis had. That was another warning for me. I devoured books day and night.

In the back rows I was checking through books on Panzer engineering and Nazi uniform design and the ruthless effectiveness of Blitzkrieg when I noticed a book with high gray chimneys that reminded me of the chimney stack of the Swastika Laundry in Dublin. I watched keenly for it on our infrequent day trips from Galway. I always tried to keep it in view from every street we walked through and kept looking behind me as we crossed busy intersections. A fifty foot swastika in red against a white background was the most striking landmark in Dublin apart from Nelson's Pillar, which the IRA blew up as part of the war on Britain.

My mother, annoyed, would push me along.

"Watch where you are going."

"Dumkoff," I'd say.

"What?"

"Watch where you are going, dumkoff. That's German for—"

"Yeah, I know. Give me a break for one day in your fucking life," she'd say.

She had a way with words. Sharp ones. Like the polished tip of fish hooks through the eyes of minnows.

The frayed book was the *Story of Auschwitz,* by Olga Lengyel. I started to read it. I picked up other books on the camps. Centerfold black and white photos. Emaciated corpses flung aside on mud rutted lanes—obscene stacks of human husks along the neat rows of barbed wire. Gauntness, hollow eyes, mass death, death huddles. Death in ditches. Diabolical creatures. Diabolical creatures who did this. Hills of shoes and spectacles. The pitiless commerce of mass killing.

I brought these books home; *Eyewitness Auschwitz: Three Years in the Gas Chambers* by Filip Muller and *Inside the Gas Chambers: Eight Months in the Sonderkommando of Auschwitz* by Shlomo Venezia. I read them in one sitting.

I went back to the Peddler and to the Galway County Library. Read about Treblinka and Sobibor and Zylon B, and Einsatzgruppen. I read about eugenics and the final solution, the Warsaw Ghetto, the experiments of Josef Mengele, injecting phenol into hearts, immersion until death in freezing water, extermination of children and adults with disabilities, the delay of the Allies in liberating the death camps, the whole squalid and lurid calculation and merciless execution of it all.

I could not assimilate the scale of what happened there. I knew there was a connection to the leaflets I received with my initiation papers but it was difficult to accept that I might be perpetuating this. I had been drawn in by the sleek uniforms, the speeding Panzers, the diving Stukas, the marshaled columns of troops. I was sucked into the apotheosis of structure and organization and fellowship because I had none of my own.

A few months later, I lay in the Regional Hospital, an emaciated husk myself, a skeletal cosmic joke of Aryan invincibility. From the hospital window I watched the tough youths from nearby Shantalla in the gardens behind their houses. I saw the Rattlesnakes stride through the concrete canyons, their bodies singing with health and purity.

My Aryan beauty scarred, shallow, seeping away. The deep red blood on crisp white sheets, a bright gleaming flag of corruption—Aryan perfection-wise. No more I skulked around Galway, the City of the Tribes, searching for the imperfect ones that would infect our tribe. The tribe was already infected.

By me.

On the ward round, Dr. Cazabon stopped at my bed. He bent down to put his cool, black palm on my pallid, glistening forehead. His clear healthy eyes scanned mine.

I looked away.

"You'll be okay," he said.

But I never was.

Listen Here to Me

I killed my stepfather when I was almost fifteen. Nobody saw it coming, especially him.

His name was Greg and I called him 'egg' because I hated them and him. Eggs come out of arseholes and Greg was Mister Arsehole. Eggs are great environments for culturing viral throwbacks. Greg was a throwback to the sixties, to mantras, to tofu sandwiches, to yoga, to pillow talk, to angst cubed, to unkemptness—if that's even a word, which I doubt, but I won't look it up, man. Greg would be proud of that 'Man' man. If his thick head wasn't at 180 degrees to where it should be. But let me backtrack.

❧

Greg was into Ki energy and bullshit. My mother fell for it. I couldn't stand for it. I met him for the first time when my mother invited him around for tea. My brother and I stood inside the hallway door as my mother introduced us. I kept looking at him with high-beam, cold eyes that my father had given me, trying to break Greg down before he even started.

"Be nice boys," my mother said.

We were. We didn't stab him in the groin, for instance.

My brother Rob just turned around and walked into the dining room. He had a searing intelligence that had begun to burn some of the neural links, so he didn't waste time on pleasantries or shit-shat as he called it. He was a laugh a minute. He studied books on mnemonics, UFOs, levitation, psychic surgery and forensic pathology.

Greg watched Rob's retreating figure and started to sweat a little. His sang-froid was out the fucking fenestre, baby! I was learning French in school so I could join the Foreign Legion.

My mother shoved past me. Pliant as always, I went with the flow and followed them into the dining room.

I knew by the way they talked it was serious. I have a sixth sense for potential disasters. If I was on hand when the Hindenburg crashed, I could have saved lives. Or at least not cried on the live broadcast from New Jersey. I thought they were supposed to be tough over there.

Tea was a fraught affair, poor chap. I said nothing to him. I only stared. Occasionally and discreetly, I stuck my tongue out when I had a full mouth of masticated Brennan's Bread. Today's Saliva Today. Meanwhile, my brother read *An Encyclopedia of Executions*.

Greg was one of those new age liberal types that I instinctively want to hatchet. I must admit he did not seem phased by my partially-dissolved bread, but I knew he had to be sweating. He tried to engage me in conversation, but I ignored him. He talked about auras, etcetera, until I was hoping that a fire from heaven would envelope him. Spontaneous combustion is rare, but maybe he was dry enough to pull it off.

Halfway through lunch, Rob stood and left the table and said nothing. Greg looked up, disconcerted, and tried to keep talking, eating, and not bursting into flames. My mother told me I could leave the table, but I just sat there absorbing as much Ki energy and bullshit as possible. They eventually finished and went into the TV room. Greg looked at me and called out "toodle-pip."

Toodle-pip? What a prick. A real greeting for ponces. His self-importance and feigned patience over-floweth. Unlike his medulla. After a few minutes, I joined them. I rarely watched TV except for *The World at War* and other documentaries on blitzkrieg or, on a lighter note, *F-Troop*,

Get Smart and *Green Acres*. Those programs were distilled genius. A bit like myself, I suppose. Agent 99 proved that women were smarter and nothing has changed my mind since. She was a good role model for the women's movement, especially since she was very smart (unlike Smart) and could use a gun. She would be perfect in a Chandler book, or one of mine, if I ever write one.

I loved Corporal Agarn in *F-Troop* and the shortsighted corporal who fell into the well at the beginning and the inept lieutenant and his girlfriend with the tassels. I could not figure out how she was attracted to him, when I was clearly available. My age and the cathode ray tube of the TV were insurmountable barriers, I suppose, but they did not curb by longing. Even Corporal Agarn was a better option for her.

I recognized Arnold the Pig as one of the better actors on TV. His owner, Mr. Haney, was a match for Ava Gabor. I loved how she threw the dishes out the window when they were finished breakfast. I tried it myself and it was a good feeling. I stole the dishes from the local hardware store for a few months. Nobody ever expected crockery to be stolen so security was lax and I had the field to myself for a while. Eventually, they redeployed their forces (I got that from *The World at War*) but by then I had moved on myself.

Anyway, my mother and Greg were whispering and sitting close together when I came in but they moved apart. "Carry on," I said and picked up the *Victor*. They had some good reconstructions of banzai charges on Iwo Jima even though I knew it backwards. At intervals I would lower the *Victor* and look over the top of the comic at the courting couple. They pretended to be watching TV but I knew their gonads were aflame like the red tips of their cigarettes. Continuing my campaign of psychological warfare, I winked when I was sure Greg made eye contact. That's ophthalmic-wise, not higher self-wise.

When *The Fugitive* started, I was interested and threw the *Victor* across the room. My mother shouted, "Victor, pick up that Victor."

I think it's fair that everyone should have a comic named after them.

"It wasn't me," I said.

"Of course it was you."

"It wasn't me."

"It was you. There's no one else here."

"What about Greg?"

"What about Greg?"

"Exactly."

"How could Greg do it? He's sitting here beside me."

"What about all that Ki energy and stuff?"

Greg looked pale and was getting paler and sweating. Spontaneous combustion was now impossible.

"Greg, don't mind him," my mother said, patting his hand.

"No problemo."

Holy God-o, I thought—as in Beckett, not the Testament.

"Greg?"

"Yes, kiddo?"

I had to admire his tenacity. He looked at me with such sincerity and openness I almost laughed. My mother seemed to relax as well.

"Greg, how does the one-armed man clean his arse?"

My mother stood and pulled me up from the floor.

"Get out of here, you crazy bastard," she said.

A tad harsh, I thought. I picked up the *Victor*. At the door, I turned.

"Toodle-pip," I said, but didn't wait for an answer.

When I got upstairs to our bedroom, Rob lay on the covers reading. I told him what happened. He laughed. I laughed as well and ran toward the bed whooping, jumped, and landed on top of him. He tickled me and wrestled me and when I fell asleep I dreamt of the one-armed man strangling Greg.

Greg came back at the weekend for another tea-time get together. While he was having tea, I went outside. I was interested in low-intensity warfare—again, courtesy of *The World at War*—so when I noticed Greg's petrol cap was loose, I decided to piss into the tank. It was difficult to piss up and produce an arc that would go into the opening, but males have an innate ability at this from centuries of practicing. They have a dominant gene for piss-arcing and flourishes. My mother called me in for tea.

"Urine, Madam?" I asked from the rear of the car.

She didn't notice that I was just finishing. She didn't wear glasses on her dates. When they came into the TV room after tea, I went out and ran through the autumnal evening full of half-light and shadows.

When I got back, Greg was standing beside his car while the AAA man hooked it up to tow it away. My mother looked dismayed and I could see Greg was annoyed.

"Bad etheric neighborhood," I said as I walked past them into the house. I ran upstairs to tell Rob. He loved it, especially the urine part, even though he then explained at length about the innate qualities of urine and its purity unless you have a kidney infection or syphilis.

"Yeah, yeah, yeah. That's great."

"Seriously, though."

"I know, Rob. Piss off."

Greg didn't come back again until they were married. Greg was a street angel and a house devil. The mantra-intoning new age façade was just that. All for show. And the façade faded fast. That's alliteration for you.

He started small.

"Listen here to me, bucko. Those whatever—Sunday roasts, baked beans, jumpers, shoes, socks, Jack's paper, etcetera—don't grow on trees, you know."

"Yeah, I know."

He hated that.

"Except coconuts," I said. "But we never seem to get

those."

He really hated that.

"Starving black babies in Africa would love that whatever—Sunday roasts, baked beans, jelly and ice cream, salmonella..."

"It's semolina actually. They have salmonella already."

He really hated that even more.

Eventually, Greg started to hit me when my mother wasn't there. I didn't respond. I took the blows and got up from the floor and faced him again. I looked into his eyes urging him to hit me. And he would. Sometimes I would sidestep his blows so gracefully I impressed myself. I showed him I could avoid them any time I wanted, but usually I let them land. I wanted to incubate that pain just like cultures humming and billowing into monsters inside nutrient-rich albumin. Did I mention I hate eggs?

Greg's reaction to me was fuelled by my ability to ignore him even when he was admonishing or hitting me. I learned not to respond to any blows. I just smiled back at him or stared into those gray Greg eyes of his.

His glancing blows to my head and ears left little evidence but were fiercely painful. His full contact punches to my back and stomach left bruises, but these were faint. When my mother finally commented on this, he attacked her.

Large fists swinging through the air, hitting her on the side of the head. Clatters, they are called in Ireland. Portent and intent enfolded into the aural effect of the word. Loud grunts from him and muted grunts from her when the blows landed and she was knocked against the door or into the TV or onto the floor. I would attack with my fists, milk bottles, the poker, a tin of baked beans.

I stuck the kitchen knife in his shoulder blade once. I had to jump up to reach. The pain was enormous, if his bellowing was any indication. Rob was away in med school cutting up cadavers, but Greg was one live body I wanted to donate to medical research. I felt my time would come. And it came the eve of my fifteenth birthday.

I was leaving my bedroom when I saw him coming out of theirs. He was stretching his arms and yawning and heading toward the bathroom. I could have done this on other occasions but my intellect always overruled me. But not today. I was going to be fifteen. Time to grow up.

As he passed the top of the stairs, I ran the length of the landing and, with a perfect two-footed flying kick, caught him in his lower back and he tumbled down the stairs without even trying to fly.

Greg realized the danger at the last minute when his peripheral vision caught a movement that was high and fast and too late. I landed on the balls of my feet at the top of the stairs—a ten, a perfect score if flying-kick, step-daddy assassination was an Olympic event. Ease of difficulty, high. I watched him tumble down the stairs, breaking the upright struts of the banister as well as his neck. It sounded like the ultimate chiropractic adjustment. He shouted in alarm as he fell, but there was no one home to hear him except me.

If he knew the least thing about aerodynamics, he might have made some minor adjustments to his flight path to save himself. However, he didn't at all.

I walked down the stairs and leaned down close so he could hear what I said.

"Listen here to me, fucko. Do you think those banisters grow on trees?"

But of course he didn't listen to me at all. He just stared up at me and blinked once or twice. Blood ran from his ear and flowed across the polished hardwood floor. The light reflected off the shiny red ribbon of blood. It pooled near the doorway.

Greg bled.

Greg's big dead head.

Blood is on the mat.

Or at least soaking into it.

And that is that.

Happy birthday, Victor.

I kicked his head and it flopped over like it belonged to a broken-necked chicken.

Eggs to eggs, arseholes to arseholes.

I shouted out "toodle-pip!" then closed the door behind me and went out into the cold, dark evening heavy with black rain clouds hugging the houses of the gray town.

The Witness

"And don't forget—no witnesses."

"Jesus, Pig. We heard you the first time," Sean answered.

John "Pig" McCann was like a broken record. No witnesses, no witnesses, no witnesses. He was financing, planning and coordinating a robbery for the following day. We were together in a room in the Galway Great Southern Hotel discussing the final run-through. His bodyguard sat with him and his driver waited outside. Sean had picked me and two others to execute the plan.

And every witness, it looked like.

✀

I didn't know Sean's other recruits, Paul Lawless and Kevin Barry, since I was a recent addition to Sean's circle. I met Sean while working in an Irish Bar in South Boston called the Banshee—on the wall were posters of Gaelic football teams, Galway Bay, the cliffs of Moher, the Rock of Cashel. Irish mob style. Irish music. Posters of poets and hunger strikers. (Sometimes, they were the same.)

The Banshee was a place full of Irish accents. German handguns. Guns in the back room. Guns in the safes. Guns in holsters. Guns in handbags. Back in Ireland, I was incarcerated in the Mercy teaching chemistry to Leaving Cert girls who were only interested in makeup and making out. I was wasting my creative energies there.

Sean usually stood at the bar counter, watching himself in the ceiling-high mirror behind the bar. Melancholy was imprinted on his face. The typical Irish tattoo. We just nodded to each other. The usual Irish embrace. He told me he was on holidays for two weeks from Galway. I had recognized him straight off from seeing him around my home city. I had total recall.

"I'm from Galway as well," I said.

"I know," he said. "Noticed you straight off."

Total recall squared.

In addition to being an habitué at the Banshee for his two weeks, I also met him on my day off at a crime fiction symposium in Boston. I was buying Ed Bunker a pint, which he told me he wasn't supposed to touch but he did anyway. I had met Ed the year before in Galway at the Cuirt Literary Festival. His French nurse wasn't too happy with me. She was blowing Gauloise smoke in my face. She was scornful.

"Irlander, huh?" she spat at me.

"Smoking's bad for votre vous, you know," I said to her.

She shrugged.

Sean walked over and joined us. He knew Bunker as well. Sean winked at the nurse. She blew smoke in his face and sauntered over to a bar stool to give us all the evil eye. She was as cute as a carcinogen. When Bunker decided to leave, we watched him walk toward the lift. The French nurse was gesticulating widely beside him.

"Jesus, she would give anyone a thirst," Sean said.

"Or an embolism," I added.

We sat together discussing Bunker, Cain, Ellroy, Hammet, Start, Oates, Woolich. After a few more hours, Sean hinted about his criminal profession. He asked me to consider it. I thought about continuing as an ineffectual teacher in the piranha-filled seas of female hooligans. I told Sean yes.

Sean told me about his ten years in South Armagh shooting British soldiers through the head trying to convince the British Army to fuck off home. He moved south to Galway and travelled to England once a month to rob building societies and banks for the IRA. He had been forced to move away from targeting banks or security van robberies in Ireland because the Irish Army and armed detectives escorted any reasonable shipment of cash. Of course the banks didn't pay for this, which I didn't like. I was a socialist at heart.

Sean thought he had one big score identified in Galway that avoided heavily armed escorts. It wasn't the usual bank, building society, or cash transit van scenario. He just hinted at first. Then elaborated. I liked it.

❧

Since I was the youngest and newest member of Sean's gang, I didn't feel I should get too involved in his debate with Pig over killing all witnesses. I knew I wasn't going to kill anyone unless it was Pig himself. He was really annoying me. I was hardwired for violence and gunplay since I was a youngster. It was a miracle I managed to go to college and get a teaching certificate. I did it to impress my mother. Irish sons will do anything to impress their mothers.

Sean explained to Pig about the disguises.

"We will be wearing masks," Sean said. "So what's the problem? What kind of witness is going to see though latex masks of Lord Lucan, Ronnie Kray, Posh Spice and David Beckham?"

We spotted the masks in a stall in East London. They would definitely cause confusion and probably paper-selling headlines.

"Lord Lucan Alive. Back as Armed Robber. Sighting Confirmed. Eye Witness Accounts page 1, 2, 4 to 25."

The tabloids are so full of shit. I am sometimes, but they are all the time.

Pig McCann was born in Belfast and raised in hell. Sometimes they can be the same. He was born with congenital syphilis, courtesy of his mother. I could easily imagine viral laden secretions slowly corrupting his brain tissue. It might explain his demeanor and thought processes. His mother pimped him to a few of her companions.

When he was sixteen, he killed three of them. The

bodies were never found. He dismembered and fed them as pig swill to one of the intensive pig farms near the border. Hence the name. The general consensus was he performed a public service and, since he was intelligent enough not to leave any traces, the RUC didn't pursue it. Even though you can be convicted without a body, it is rare. Belfast was in chaos at the time so no one was too bothered really.

I was glad to be a vegetarian when I heard about the pig story. I don't eat meat, smoke or drink, so I expect to live a charmed life. So far so good. But this caper might change that.

Pig joined the INLA and earned a living from extortion, drugs, armed robbery and killing pedophiles, Brits, and rival INLA faction members on the side. He did fairly well but eventually he was convicted to Long Kesh for ten years on the supergrass evidence of Martin Kelly. Graffiti appeared in Belfast during that time.

"I knew Martin Kelly. Thank fuck he didn't know me."

When Pig was released he went to Dublin, left the INLA, but took their innate view of crime and punishment with him, i.e. mercenary and merciless. He started his own gang and was adamant that he did not want anyone to be able to identify him ever again at the scene of a crime. He would only direct operations and not execute them. Sean was his oldest friend from Belfast and was the only one of us who felt safe talking back to him.

"I don't give a fuck what you wear," McCann was shouting. "Don't leave any witnesses."

"It doesn't make sense," Sean tried to reason with him. "There could be six or eight people there. If you kill them, there will be fucking mayhem. There is no way the Gardaí will let it lie."

Pig said nothing.

"It's not like up north—killing Prods by the van load or Taigs in pubs and betting shops," Sean said. "Nobody gives a fuck about that, really. It's tit for tat. But the Gardaí have to hunt us down if we massacre half a dozen upstanding citizens. It's a challenge to the Irish State."

Pig blew cigarette smoke toward Sean.

"It's like Foot and Mouth—they will eradicate us no matter what," Sean said.

Anything that might damage tourism is dealt with ruthlessly except dog shit on the streets and a few other anomalies; bankers, developers, corrupt politicians.

"Unless there are a bunch of refugees working there you can forget about getting away with it," Sean said.

Pig pounded the table. Five handguns and five glasses of water (it was high summer) rattled. Three glasses fell over. Everyone grabbed the guns to keep the spreading water from contaminating them.

"Sean is right," I said after a brief lull.

Pig looked at me.

"What?"

"Sean's right. No one can see through those masks."

"Who the fuck are you to tell me what to do? You could be a fucking pig for all I know."

"You have a thing about pigs," I said.

Sean laughed.

Pig looked at me sharply. His bodyguard looked up. Paul and Kevin smirked.

"The only reason you're here is because of Sean's say so, you college educated prick," Pig said.

"That's college educated prick, Bachelor of Science, First in Class, First Class Honors in Chemistry, if you don't mind. And I'm not too happy about you either," I continued, much to my own and everyone else's amazement.

They all looked at me.

Pig squinted for a long time, then looked at Sean and laughed.

"That college educated fucker has balls anyway."

The tension was lifted but so was the safety on my pistol just in case.

"I don't give a fuck how many witnesses there are, so long as there are none when you leave. We'll be long gone before they can figure it out."

"Okay, okay," Sean said, but I didn't believe he was serious.

"Any other questions?" Pig asked the rest of us.

He looked at me a while but his gaze moved on to the others. No one said anything. I lifted a glass of water to my lips and half choked as I swallowed. Not very sophisticated really. Everyone laughed. It was nervous laughter. But it was okay.

"Let's go and get a result then," Pig said. "We'll meet at the Dublin Airport Hotel—you know the room—in four weeks time to share the money and don't forget..."

"No witnesses," I said.

"Maith an fear," he said. (Good man.) "Go to the top of the class."

"I was there already."

Everyone laughed.

We stood up and holstered our weapons.

I shook hands with Paul and Kevin. It was like they were leaving town even though I would see them early the next morning. But you never know in this business. Here today, dead tomorrow. Like Sean and Pig, they were both from Belfast—reliable, good with guns and crowds, abduction, hijacking, driving, escapes and women. I was the only Southern and sometimes found it difficult to unravel the conversations they had when they spoke rapid fire to each other.

They were in a different hotel to me and Sean. They left the room first and we waited ten minutes.

Myself, Sean, Pig and his bodyguard left together. Outside, his driver approached and waited at a discreet distance as we prepared to separate. Pig watched the street and his reflection in car windows. A bit of a poseur, I thought, but I can't talk. I wear an ankle bracelet.

Pig got into his car. Sean walked over to me.

"He has a thing about witnesses," Sean said and laughed.

I had to admire the plan, though. It was a good plan. It would be a brilliant plan if it worked.

℘

Where: The Tote at Galway Racecourse.

When: Following afternoon during the Galway Plate.

Why: €2,000,000.

Who: Pig (planner/financier/non-combatant).

Sean Rowley (lead man/recruiter/grenades/Semtex).

Paul Lawless (second in command/guards/Armalite).

Kevin Barry (alarms/CCTV/Luger).

James McGowan (me/doors/timing/Luger).

Extra people in Galway: 50,000—city strangled with traffic, tourists, bookies, pickpockets, beggars, street traders, McDonalds happy meal wrappers and every spare Garda in the land.

The split: €2,000,000 total. Minus €500,000 for Pig = (€1,500,000 /4) = €375,000 each.

Extra insurance: Simultaneous robbery at a poker game in the Galway Bay Hotel in Salthill by the Laffey gang who had flamboyant tendencies, i.e. spray and pray. They loved to show off. Hopefully, it would draw all the Gardaí from the racecourse.

Real gamblers stay on track by avoiding the race track and playing cards all day and night during race week. But this is one time they should have joined the rest of the population in Ballybrit. Even the University gets two half days for the races. That's what I call a liberal education.

℘

Myself and Sean headed back to the Skeffington Arms. I didn't know where Paul and Kevin stayed, nor they us. We had all arrived in Galway the previous weekend on various trains. The July sun was shining all weekend. A minor miracle for Galway. We were able to wear sunglasses without comment because so was everyone else.

64

We went for a meal in Nimmo's and then walked around the City. Quay Street was almost impassable with drinkers and visitors. I could smell money and the sweet aroma of sunburned female flesh. James Ellroy eat your angst-eaten liver out (or whatever it is this week).

We sat outside Café De Journal drinking tea while overweight, over-pampered race goers walked up and down Quay Street. We free-wheeled through the job for the next day. We knew everything about the racecourse, the escape routes, the roads, the fields and the nearby housing estates.

At intervals, helicopters flew low overhead taking the nouveau riche to the racecourse from hotels around the city, drowning out all conversation. It reminded me of Vietnam footage. Their rotors evoked in me a strange melancholy. Talk about emotionally labile. In Vietnam, helicopters ferried overly-laden nervous grunts. Here, it was smarmy, overweening business suits.

I know the helicopters affected Sean because he was once thrown blindfolded out of a British Army helicopter in South Armagh. It was only a few feet off the ground, but he didn't know. If they hadn't done that to him, he wouldn't have ended up shooting their comrade's brains out from a thousand yards away. The Brits wonder then why no one likes them.

His conversation was not very linear whenever another one flew over Quay Street. We shaded our eyes and looked up and tracked each flight until they passed from view. After each interruption it was difficult to resume our previous conversation even if it only covered topics like alarms and how we would spend the money.

We went back to the Skeff early to rest and sleep if possible. I was sorry to leave all that blistering female skin behind though.

I slept through the night and woke at 6:00. We didn't eat breakfast at the hotels, but met in different cafes; Lynch's, the GBC, LydonHouse, Nimmo's. At midday, we caught buses from Eyre Square to the Ballybrit racecourse along with all the other peasants who weren't going by helicopter.

We travelled on different buses.

At 2:45 in the afternoon, carloads of Gardaí left the Racecourse. The Laffeys were in motion.

We went into motion.

At 3:00, the big race started, the Galway Plate. We put on our masks and moved from the enclosure area toward the rear of the Tote entrance, guarded by three security men and a plainclothes detective.

Sean in his Lord Lucan mask stuck a pistol in the detective's ear and got them all to lie on the ground. The three security guys were on the ground before we even finished the order, but the detective was hesitant until we hit him behind the ear with his own gun. We tied their arms behind them with flexi-cuffs and taped their mouths.

One minute gone.

I shouted out "One minute gone. Six minutes left."

We crouched on the ground while Sean set a small C4 charge with a ten-second fuse—time is money, you know—followed by a discreet, low volume blast that dislodged the reinforced door. Before the Tote staff could react, Sean threw in two blast grenades and we ripped the door off its hinges and rushed in, pulling the security guards and the real Guard with us. We pushed them to the ground just inside the door, face down.

Total chaos.

Everyone was screaming or crying or staring.

We fired into the ceiling and monitors showing the race. We blew the lights and visual displays to smithereens. Everyone stopped screaming. I beckoned them to the ground. They did.

Kevin had ten seconds to disable the CCTVs and alarm system before the police were alerted, but they weren't even activated. Jesus, they wouldn't do that again in a hurry. He jumped the counter.

"Three minutes gone," I shouted. "Four minutes left."

Money everywhere.

I counted eight clerks with their hands behind their heads. Two of them were women—but they had no blistered skin so I ignored them.

I shouldn't have.

We threw the canvas bags over the counter and Sean and the others started to fill them. I was still watching the door and the money pile up and the Galway Plate on the only monitor that hadn't been hit. I heard footsteps running from outside through the door we blasted open. I dropped to my knee.

The footsteps didn't stop. I aimed at the center of the doorway and prepared to earn my cut. Pig appeared in the doorway. Fuck, I nearly shot him.

I should have.

"What the fuck are you doing here?" I said.

"Take it easy. I just wanted to see what's happening. I miss the action."

Talk about fickle. He didn't have a mask either, but no cameras were recording and everyone was face down so it wasn't too bad. He strode passed me.

"It's me," he roared. The others turned around but only for a few seconds and turned back to keep filling the bags.

"Five minutes gone," I shouted. "Two minutes left."

Pig sauntered up and down past the Tote workers sprawled around the floor huddled together and shaking. He carried an Armalite in one hand. Pig noticed the two women. He walked up to the nearest one and lifted her skirt with the rifle.

"Pig, knock it off," I said.

I was in the Boy Scouts when I was a kid. Some things don't wear off.

"Don't talk to me, college boy, if you know what's good for you," he said without even turning around.

"Leave her alone—we don't have time for this," I said

and then raised my voice. "Six minutes gone. One minute left. Finish up."

Pig turned and smiled at me.

"You a homo or something?" he said. "I like these two." He gestured at the women on the floor. He had his head turned toward me.

One of the women suddenly jumped to her feet. She had a stiletto in her fist and stabbed Pig in the shoulder. He discharged a round in reflex and blood spurted onto the floor from a terrible wound inflicted on the other woman still lying down. Blood and globules of pink tissues slowly trailed across the floor toward my feet. I pulled the woman with the stiletto off Pig and pushed her away. She dropped to the floor to attend the other woman. What the fuck was she doing with a knife was all I could think of. Pig pulled the knife from his shoulder. And then he bent down and stabbed her in the temple and left it there. Why was I surprised?

I would have shot Pig but didn't want to leave any evidence behind. The woman fell over onto her side with bright aerated blood spurting from her head. I shot her in the heart to stop it pumping. The energy of the place had changed completely. Anything could happen. And of course it did.

Who said chivalry was dead? The three security guards and the real Garda decided to rush us even though their hands were tied. A real kamikaze charge. I shot the four of them. I aimed for their legs but hit them all about midriff so they would soon be in agony. I was a bit tense, hence the bad aim.

Meanwhile, Pig was firing a full clip into the woman attacker even though she was past caring. I could see the family resemblance of both women as they lay there dead together, their blood coalescing on the smooth tiled floor. I recognized, then—cousins of the Laffey's. We would be on the run forever.

"They're fucking Laffeys, you know. We are so fucked," I said and checked my watch. "Zero minutes," I called out.

"Let's go."

"What the hell are they doing working here?" Pig asked.

"Who knows?" I said. "Maybe these two had gone straight."

"Carrying a stiletto? I don't think so," Pig said.

"Old habits die hard."

"Everyone dies hard," he said.

I said nothing more.

Pig was crazed. He loaded another clip and walked over to the guards. He fired at them until the clip was empty.

Sean was raging. I could see from the way he walked. He started screaming at Pig but Pig just shrugged. I couldn't hear what Sean said. My ears were reverberating with the sound of screams and gunfire.

Pig must have decided he had done enough in the witness elimination program because he ignored the terrified staff on the floor that were huddled together trying to avoid the growing pool of blood inching toward them. Sean dropped one of the canvas bags at my feet. It made a splashing sound in the blood. I holstered the pistol and lifted the bag.

Jesus I could barely lift it. We're in the money, I thought.

And deep shit, obviously.

I went to the door and checked the exit. It was clear. I could hear sirens approaching but they were muted by the shouts from the crowd as the big winner of the Galway Plate came home. We were the real winners though. The bag was so heavy I was sweating. We tried to stay low, but Pig walked flamboyantly beside us with his Armalite held high in the air, the butt against his hip. Talk about grandstanding. Some people noticed and ducked and some stood transfixed and one or two lifted their mobiles.

Pig fired in their direction and they fell to the ground.

We walked past the Dignitary's Car Park and entered the helicopter parking zone.

Did you guess it?

We walked to the Bell People Carrier that we booked

earlier with a stolen credit card. The pilot was sitting inside, reading *The Guards* by Ken Bruen. Sean pulled him out and we heaved the bags in and then got in. Kevin started the rotors. He had been a pilot in the American Army for five years. Pig shot the pilot who was looking in at us. The bullet went through *The Guards*.

What a day. It was a hardcover, so he might make it.

The helicopter dipped as we lifted off, but then Kevin righted it. As we rose, Pig took aim at the crowds below us and mimicked shooting at them. Such a trickster.

He was one pork belly with a poor future. I was sweating after the adrenalin rush and the run to the helicopter. I had to start visiting the gym again. We flew high and into the West. We could see police cars stuck in traffic below us. Traffic in both directions was miles long and barely moving.

We flew out past Maam Cross. No radar coverage out there, just gorse bushes and spindly trees sheltering against the Atlantic winds. We flew over the only Fjord in Ireland. (The Queen of Connemara—four sailings daily during the summer, starting at €15 for adults which includes tea, coffee, scones, light snacks and the best toilets on the ocean, apparently.)

We flew onwards past Clifden. After six miles out into the Atlantic, we headed south toward the Burren where we had cars waiting. We would keep out of radar contact all the way. We flew low over the sea. Each of us dumped our gloves, overalls and masks into individual weighted canvas sacks. Pig stood at the hatch and flung each one as far as he could.

"Try lifting prints off of those," he kept saying. He must be reliving stone throwing on the Falls Road or throwing crunchy fragments of his tormentors to the pigs. He had a look of serenity on his face that I hadn't seen before.

As I passed my weighted sack to him, I held it for a minute and we looked at each other. His look of serenity began to fade. He was about to. I pulled my Luger and shot him in the chest. Everyone jumped.

Except Pig. He managed to hold on to the door frame, but he looked surprised.

His Armalite was nearby but if he let go to grab it gravity would grab him.

"No witnesses," I said. "You're the only one that can be identified."

I looked over at Sean. He nodded.

Kevin looked back at me from the pilot's seat. I indicated a tilting gesture with my hand. He nodded and then slowly tilted the helicopter so that Pig's grasp faltered. His rifle slid across the metal floor and hit him on the head as it soared into the Atlantic. Jesus, he still held on. He was mostly outside the helicopter now, just holding on with two monstrous arms. I never noticed them before. I fired a shot into the top of his head. An unusual angle. It split open. I never saw him move so elegantly as he fell in slow motion.

Pigs can fly after all.

I sat on the floor of the helicopter with my legs dangling out the hatch, the July sun cascading off the blue ocean of the Atlantic, the limestone of the Burren clean and white and pure, the rotors above me soothing as I watched the Pig go down on Galway Bay.

The Perfect Son

"Hi, Ma."

She gave me a big hug and started to cry.

"It's okay, Ma, it's okay."

She broke the embrace, held my hand and brought me in.

"Let me have a look at you."

That must be a quote implanted in every Irish mother at birth. It made me uncomfortable.

"Where is he?"

"Upstairs. He's sleeping now, so let him rest."

"Don't worry. I'm in no hurry to see him."

"Ahh, don't be like that now."

"Okay, Ma. We'll have some tea so?"

The Irish solution to every crisis and lacuna of awkwardness.

I left my duffel bag on the hall floor and followed her into the kitchen and watched her body, sculpted now by constant worry and fatigue. She still had strong hair. Wiry, thick, sleek. It was cut short and mostly black. I wanted to reach out and touch it.

She had the characteristic good looks of her sisters, but not the good grace to marry well like them. She had high cheek bones and blue-green eyes—they reflected a deep ocean emptiness I remembered from when I left twenty years before.

The same patterned wallpaper in the hallway was faded and blemished. It filled me with despair and reverie. A deep burnished sheen of pain sliced into me over the life my mother had spent since I left.

"When did you get back?"

"A couple of weeks ago, but I had to do a few things first. Sorry I didn't ring or anything."

"That's okay. As long as you got the message."

"It took a while to reach me. How is he?"

"He's pretty bad. He doesn't really know me all the time. It's hard."

"Does he ever talk about me?"

She hesitated, but I knew he didn't and so changed the subject.

"And how are you, Ma? You look tired."

"I'm okay really but I'm glad you're here. You look strong. I like the shaved head, but it makes you look scary."

"It's kind of a sacrificial thing. It's hard to explain."

"That's okay. It sort of makes sense. It suits the shape of your head."

"Thanks, I think. It's funny. You never mind anything, whereas the old man can't stand me."

"That's not right, really. He just couldn't understand, that's all."

"Ma, I know he loathes me, but it's okay. I got over it a long time ago."

That's why I'm so successful now in my chosen profession, blessed with an aptitude and high tolerance for heights, suffering, and number-one haircuts. No CAO application or Leaving Cert points scrabble.

"He had a hard life, you know, and if you saw him now you wouldn't be angry for long."

"We'll see. I'm here anyway. That's the main thing."

"Yes it is. Thanks for coming. I know what I asked of you is a lot."

"It's no problem, Ma. That water is boiling. Sit down and I'll make the tea. Jesus you look wrecked, Ma."

"Okay, yes. I'm so tired. My back is sore all the time.

I'll sit just for a while. I want to talk to you as well. I didn't know if you were alive or not until last year. I thought of you every day."

"Okay, Ma. We'll talk soon. I'll make that tea first."

It took me a while to find the tea bags. Cobwebs decorated the cupboards. I poured the water and let it sit and found some Mikado biscuits and when I came back she was sleeping in the chair. I was startled. She looked dead. I could see shallow breathing when I knelt down beside her. She still had the olive skin and regal look of her mother. She sighed at intervals. I checked her pulse. It was weak but steady.

I poured a cup for myself and went out to the back garden to have a cigarette. The sky was clear. It was a cold winter night with a full moon. I was often locked out here for minor reasons—not being quiet or studious or not being the perfect son, whatever that is. On those nights, I heard my mother crying in the kitchen arguing with my father and knew I wouldn't cry. And I never did.

I developed strategies to ignore my father, which incensed him. He hit me, he punched me, he complained about me, he berated me, he mimicked me, he shouted at me, he threatened me, he ignored me, he locked me out, he knocked me out and I grew stronger each time I absorbed his anger and transmuted it into fearlessness and into a body and mind bereft of emotion. I killed him in my heart each day and eventually he felt it.

I finished the cigarette and flicked it into the garden, watching the red glow cartwheel through the air like a rogue incendiary device. It reminded me of nights bivouacked in Algiers, the Dacca Valley and the Mekong Delta. Exotic names I read long before in comic books. Adventure tales made manifest. Make believe murdered. Child fantasy fermented into foulness.

Those Viet Cong fuckers weren't as good as people make out. We ambushed them in paddy fields and temples and in the tunnels and wore their severed ears around our necks.

I walked inside and locked the back door. My mother still slept. Her tea was untouched and I picked it up and threw it into the sink. I left the kitchen, walked through to the hallway and stood listening for a few moments at the bottom of the stairs.

What was I expecting to hear? I know I often listened to determine if he was waiting in the dark for me on the landing or in one of the rooms off of it, ready to ambush me. It reminded me of that scene in Psycho when the detective is attacked on the landing by Mrs. Bates. I jump every time. What a mover. That's the only scene that bothers me from any horror film.

"Okay," I said to myself. "Just get up there will you?"

I went up there (taking my chances), and headed for my parents' room. I saw the outline of his body and moved closer. I opened a window for some air, but it made little difference. It smelled bad. I could hear shallow rapid breaths.

"Well, Daddio. You're not dead yet, I see. Getting things your way as usual."

I watched him for a while and tried to forgive him but it wasn't going to happen. The impulse was transient. It lasted nanoseconds. I wasn't really the forgiving kind. It wasn't possible, so no use wasting any more time on it. I tried to take into account he never finished primary school, worked hard every day, married into a wealthy intellectual family which caused him bouts of intense unease and inferiority and he never drank. He didn't smoke either, since I was born.

In the deficit column, the weight of his actions were enough to sink the Graff Spree. End of audit. Even in terms of smoking I could not award any merits because he was a smoker when I was conceived—imagine how far I might have soared without that nicotine-tainted booster rocket at kick off.

I blamed Dr. Benjamin Spock as well. He didn't warn parents that smoking was not an aid to healthy sperm production. He never advised physical and mental abuse as an aid to better parenthood either but Daddio certainly embraced that concept with fervor. I wondered if the Spock fucker was still alive and who else was blaming him. I might check if he was still alive and go from there.

I remember once on the landing he whacked me on the back of the head and, since I was running past already, the extra momentum carried me off the ground over the banister and hurtled me through the air until I landed on the narrow stairs, breaking my leg and arm and fracturing my skull. As a result, I later developed a perverse taste for free-fall, so I was perfect for a paratrooper career. I was always first to volunteer to drop blindfolded prisoners out of helicopters. I was free-falling emotionally and psychically long before this. My leg hurts whenever the weather is rainy. My head always hurts, but that's not from the fall.

He never apologized for anything he said or did or left undone, so there you go.

I shook him awake, not gently.

"Hey, wake up. Guess who?"

He tried to focus. I knew he was in severe pain because Ma told me and I saw him flinch. He had difficulty focusing due to the medication and a cataract. I noticed the occlusions.

"Who is that?"

"Well it's not an angel, so don't worry. You're still here."

"Is that the doctor?"

"Not exactly."

"Who's there? I can't see. Is the window open? Jesus it's cold in here."

"Well, it won't be where you're going."

"Who is that? Where's Ma?"

"It's your only rotten son. You know, the airborne one."

He missed a few breaths and stared up at me in the darkness.

"Any crack?" I said.

"Is that you?"

"In person."

"I thought I'd never see you again."

"Likewise, but you can't have everything your way all the time."

"Why are you here?"

"Is that any way to greet me? You never change. How come a fucker like you is still breathing?"

His eyes closed.

"Wake up. I'm talking to you."

I pulled out a Luger and tapped his teeth to get his attention.

It worked.

"You see this? I ought to blow your heart out if you have one."

He was sweating and staring at me, eyes fully dilated cataract or not. Mind over matter, obviously.

"This is why I'm here," I said, nodding toward the weapon.

He tried to call out for my mother as usual but I pushed the pistol into his mouth.

"She's wrecked. Leave her be. You've called her for the last time."

I chambered a round.

He squeezed his eyes closed and cried.

"Anyway it was her who asked me to come."

She did, but only to ease his suffering and give him a painless death, but no need to tell him that. I am sure his higher self knew this when it occupied his body at birth, so it wasn't my problem if he had forgotten.

He looked shocked. I had his attention now, for sure.

"She wanted to be rid of you. Do you know what you did to her and to me?"

I could feel the rage suppressed for years in carefully crafted silos moving to launch position. I had to calm down. I didn't want to go overboard. That wouldn't do. I breathed deeply. It wasn't easy. I was sweating and shaking. "Jesus," I said a few times. I could feel the cold night air through the open window, evoking many nights shaking from the cold out in the back garden. I realized that the gun was moving aimlessly in his mouth.

He was fully awake now.

"Anything to say? Don't shout."

I took the pistol out. I would have to clean it later. His mouth was filthy.

"You're not my son."

"Is that it? Jesus, how original. Why did you bother?"

I pushed the gun back in before he bored me to death.

I pulled a small silver case from my jacket pocket and opened it. He looked at it and at me.

The moonlight shone off the syringe. A real cinematic moment, actually. Hopefully, a director will read this.

He tried to struggle, but his strength was ebbing. It was hardly worth a mercy killing, but it was a request from my mother. She never asked for anything. I listened to hear if she was moving around downstairs.

When I was sure she was still asleep, I injected the dose into his arm. He mounted a more vigorous resistance to this, but it was futile. I was pushing my weight down on him while pushing the gun into his mouth.

I waited. I waited for it.

He bucked off the bed. His face and mouth contorted from the cyanide ions scavenging every oxygen molecule— the strength of these contortions are always stunning, even from an emaciated body like his. I had to clamp my hand over his mouth because some inarticulate sounds were creeping past the barrel of the Luger. His legs were bouncing off the bed so I had to lie on top of him. What a fuss. After about five minutes—good average—his body was still.

It was not a mercy killing, really.

It was a merciless killing really.

It was a killing really.

It was good. Really.

I sat there and smoked a cigarette and blew smoke in his face. It would have driven him crazy. There is nothing an ex-smoker hates more. I should have included it in the support act before the main performance.

I sat there for another while and thought I would feel some ease, but felt nothing at all.

I went downstairs and sat in the kitchen opposite my mother. After a short while she woke up and looked at me. I nodded. She cried and I held her hand.

"Was it painless?"

"Yes, Ma. Don't worry. It was fine."

"Did he wake?"

"No."

"Thanks for that. I know it was hard thing for you to do."

It wasn't that hard really.

All in the Mind

When we saw movement through the spyhole, Jacko kicked the door in. It was red. It was flimsy. It was number fucking fifty. A five story walk up, a total dump on West 189th Street, Washington Heights. We fucking walked up.

Jacko wore steel-tipped Doc Martin boots he stole in Grafton Arcade when Boot Boys ruled Dublin okay? When we carried machetes and razors. When gaunt Alsatians loped beside us like feral guardians, tethered to us with silver and leather chains. When we wore black parallels and skinhead haircuts. When we wore thin bomber jackets all shiny and new. When we were all shiny and new. When we dated high cheeked Comanche girls from Fatima Mansions who caused mayhem, who carried blades for us, who cut up Dublin Four girls, who raced with us through the rain-sleeked Dublin Streets.

The Corporation estates of Dublin sired us. Sheriff Street weaned us. Our blood lines honed by generations of Saxons, Normans, Black and Tans, the Dublin Fusiliers, by the topography of carnage that was the Western Front, the Crimea, Kyber Pass, the Congo, Lebanon.

Pirates once our forefathers were. Snipers once we were. Soldiers true once we were. Heroes once we were for the Kings and Queens of England, for Dublin Castle. Now heroin found us, bound us, gagged us, laid us down on the hard Dublin concrete. Laid us down to wrest.

Just me and Jacko made it. Made it to New York to Woodlawn, in the high North of the Bronx. No one wore

Doc Martens in New York except avant-garde NYU types. In the summer most people wore flip flops, including Dominican gangsters across the Harlem River in Upper Manhattan. Here we were in DR land looking for clues and money and trouble.

The door flew open. The skimpy chain and lock catapulted through the air and hit the hardwood floor. So did the guy inside who lost his balance, arms wind-milling while he tried to stay upright. As he lifted his head, Jacko kicked him in the temple.

We came in and closed the door. The jamb was a bit askew. So were we. The whole place was a dump. The guy sat on the floor rubbing his head. Jacko pulled him up by the hair, the guy protesting, trying to pull loose as he scrambled to his feet. Jacko pushed him back toward the sofa that was covered in cushions and throw rugs. Motes of dust flowered up to the ceiling.

I rushed over to open the window.

"Jacko, go easy on that fucking mushroom dust cloud. My asthma is bad enough already."

"Asthma my arse. It's all in the mind," he said.

"I suppose anaphylactic shock is all in the mind as well."

"What?"

"You know. Deadly allergic reaction to shellfish or peanuts or culchies. Like when the victim turns blue and bloated and dies in agony in front of you."

"Peanuts my arse," Jacko said.

I looked down at our victim.

"Pedro, what's arse in Spanish?"

I was just curious, you know.

This neighborhood was all Spanish speakers from the Dominican Republic (DR land, see above). They spat on the streets, on the subways, on the stairwells, on platforms, on escalators. Just like the Irish a hundred years ago.

I was allergic to germs of all ethnic origins, not to mention dust motes. I should have worked in the Public

Health arena where I could get paid for enforcing my zero tolerance of slack food preparation standards, of cross contamination, of molds, of vermin, of sneezes, of spits.

"Who fucking cares?" Jacko said, turning to the Dominican on the couch. "Where is the fucking money from Croke Park?" Jacko asked, punching him in the face.

Every Irishman in Woodlawn came to the Croke Park bar to remember home, turf smoke, Atlantic swells, mournful cries of seagulls, the All-Ireland Finals, Italia '90, climbing the Reek, and sleeting rain racing in from the Atlantic. They watched themselves in the long mirror behind the bar, hunkered down like desperate jockeys, bleak, broken, broken-veined, ready to drink themselves to a standstill. Ready to fight, to feel the pain, to hit the deck from an uppercut or a haymaker, to alleviate the misery they could not articulate or fathom. Full fathom five thy misery lies, Mister Irishman.

These Dominicans had robbed the Croke Park in broad nightlight, when half of Woodlawn was still awake.

The Irish don't follow the early to bed, early to rise motto of the Americans. The Irish would go to bed at five in the morning and be up at seven to work on the building sites, firing nailguns at each other to keep alert in case they walked out into clean space and smashed their bodies on the hard concrete thirty stories below

The Dominicans broke in three hours after closing time and straight into a bar full of Dublin supporters who had just lost to Meath (again) at the real Croke Park. They rushed the raiders, who managed to stay calm and fired into the crowd. Dubs were falling over themselves to reach the Dominicans since there were no Meath men around even though the four Domincans had handguns and the Dubs could barely stand from the drink. If only they had their nailguns with them, it would have been an even match.

The Dominicans stayed calm enough to take the till receipts, but they looked scared and dropped half of the money on the way out. They used so much ammo they had to reload. No Irish got killed. It was luck and the physical dexterity that one acquires after drinking all day. It's in the genes, Mister.

"Jacko," I said. "You know what? Jacko might be a Dominican name. Pedro, Ricardo, Rodrigo, Salivo, Spito, Jacko, etcetera."

"Very droll."

He had a good vocabulary for an ex-Boot Boy. Like myself. None of the others in our group made it. All graduates of Mountjoy, summa cum laudanum. Injecting into veins, in their feet and groin. All the long summers gone, sucked back into oblivion like the blood cloud sucked back into the hypodermic from those shriveled veins.

"What do you think, Pedro? Is Jacko your Dublin cousin?" I asked.

The Domincan was dazed. He kept looking back and forth at us during our verbal exchanges trying to make sense of what was happening.

"Qué?" he said.

"Don't start with the qué shit," Jacko said, punching him again, and again he fell back on the sofa. "This is not *Fawlty Towers.*"

More dust. I moved away. I moved to the window where I could breathe better. I looked out on Saint Nicholas Avenue. A goddamn hellhole. It was like the Irish ghettoes of the lower east side a hundred years ago. At least we were all Catholics, I supposed, but since I was lapsed it didn't help.

I was lapsed since I put Father O'Shea into the Royal Canal with a Calor Gas cylinder wrapped around his ankles. I could see him under the gray still water, his cassock floating over his head like a hovering black stingray. I saw one once in the aquarium in Galway. Father O'Shea was there floating upright for a month until his ankles came loose and his feet dropped to the canal floor tied to the yellow Calor Gas anchor. He didn't pop to the surface, but he made it half way and lay horizontally for a week or so until a policeman noticed him. The papers went wild. But he was asking for it, so he got it. He was an informer, a Garda arse-wiper, a big fat baby, a holy joe, a holy show, a fucking pedophile, a swarmy namby pamby sugar dandy. Where was I?

Jacko went into the kitchen to search the place. And wreck it. He flung everything from the fridge onto the floor. He sailed frozen pizzas like Frisbees through the air into the living room. He stomped avocados into pieces and gore. He pulled the door off the fridge and threw it across the kitchen. He pulled the freezer door off its hinges. He pulled every drawer open and broke them and flung them in a pile. He was happy.

He went into the bedroom and thrashed it. He went into the bathroom and smashed it. He came back into the living room and lost it. He pulled Pedro up and headbutted him in the face. Blood burst out like a pomegranate thrown against a concrete floor.

"Jacko, go easy," I said.

"Go easy, my arse. This fucker knows something."

All he knew, I thought at this stage, was he wished he knew something. He was mumbling and bleeding and crying like a baby.

"Pedro, baby, stop crying or I'll get rough," Jacko said.

Someone knocked on the door.

"Pedro. Pedro?"

Followed by silence.

We pulled our revolvers out. I preferred them to automatics although they were slower but we never missed so it wasn't a problem. Pity we weren't at Croke Park when the DR boys arrived.

"His fucking name is Pedro," I whispered to Jacko. "Can you believe it?" I tapped Pedro on the head with the barrel of my pistol. He didn't like it.

Pedro looked like he was going to cry out so Jacko kicked him.

His head flew back and hit the hardwood floor.

He was out.

The guns were out.

Outside, the woman stopped knocking and started speaking and we could hear her heavy breathing between sentences. After a short time, she pushed a note under the door.

Jacko went over to retrieve it. He listened at the door before picking it up.

"Fuck. It's in Pedronese." He passed it to me

"It's okay," I said. "There's an address. Maybe the money is there."

We heard a noise behind us. Pedro was getting to his feet. He was pulling a shotgun from under the couch, fumbling it, sweating it, blood dripping on the dark gray barrels. Before he could level it, aim it, cock it, fire it, Jacko was over there. He jumped the couch and threw his revolver to me. I caught it as it came toward me, butt over barrel. Jacko grabbed both barrels of the shotgun. He started swinging. Pedro held on. Jacko kept spinning and so did Pedro, who kept trying to put his finger around the trigger.

Jacko should have been in the Olympics. The centrifugal force made Pedro lose his grip. He stumbled across the room until his legs collided against the window ledge and he toppled backward out the open window. He tried to grab the edge of the window frame but he was moving too quickly. We could hear his body hitting the hard metal of the fire escape and then a sharp silence as he fell outward until he hit the basement courtyard five floors below.

"Jesus, did you see that? Your fucking asthma came in handy after all," Jacko said.

Jacko had a warped sense of humor.

"Okay, let's wipe the barrels and toss it out the window," I said. "They might figure he stumbled and fell."

It wasn't very realistic since the place was wrecked, but maybe they would buy it.

Jacko wiped the barrels with a dishcloth and tossed the

gun out the window. He didn't look down. He was afraid of heights.

I felt like telling him it was all in the mind.

As we pulled the door shut behind us, a woman's scream rose through the hot humid air.

Killing the Laffeys

We left the Banshee at dusk, the police in unmarked cars out front, smoking, on cell phones, working hard as usual, black bunting pinned to the front door, the smell of cordite from the previous night lingering still.

Three guys strolled in near midnight, firing handguns, two in each hand, a bit overblown, six six-guns, nondescript pinched faces, wiry, in jeans, in firing stances. The place was packed. Saturday night. Irish. Irish Americans. Boys. Girls. Families. Then the three fuckers blasting. Bodies and blood flying. Screaming. Trays and glasses smashing. Teeming blood. Two waiters dying. Head wounds. I killed the attackers. Their guns dry firing in harmony. Amateur hour. I stood up from an upturned table and let them have it. They had it coming.

I thought I left the killings behind in Belfast. The killings in sweet shops, in taxis, in cafes, in hotels, in snugs, in the Holy Land, in Divis, in Ballymurphy, in hospital waiting-rooms, in abandoned sheds, in culverts, in lush pastures, in narrow country-lanes, at crossroads, at creameries, on high-ways, on hillsides, in grottos, in churches, in graveyards, in high-rise tenements, in the back of Saracens, on the wet macadam. In person, in the dark, in the back, in the back of the head—callous, calculated, no mercy, no quarter, no rules, no honor.

It followed me to Boston, where the Irish run deep, where blood runs deep, where my cousins live, where they run the Banshee, where they run the remnants of a '60s

Irish gang founded by my uncle, Tom Rowley, my mother's brother.

At home in Ireland, I saw him on long ago summer days, saving turf, standing in the rushes, stripped to his waist, the scars of healed bullet wounds puckering his back. The sun high, his muscles taut and working rhythmically, beads of sweat flying from his torso as he dug into the wet heavy peat and flung the sods onto the bank high above him. I watched the wounds, wondered how they felt, felt proud he was my uncle. Wanted to touch those keratinized, pale gray wounds.

When he heard the sound of an unfamiliar car approach, he crouched low, relaxed, waiting, unafraid but wary, watching me. When it passed, he looked over, winked and stood again stretching his limbs. He was a gentleman. And a gunman, of course. The women loved him. He didn't see them. When they called the house he handed the phone to my mother. "He is busy right now," she would say, blowing blue-gray smoke into the air.

Now my uncle was stretched out in hospital. Alive. Still fighting back. Shiny slick slivers of bullet fragments meshed in his brain, folded into the cocoon of tissue and vessels. Black sutures in his shaved skull, purple-blue bruises the color of rotten fruit high in his forehead, liquids flowing sluggishly along the opaque tubes through the rough aperture the paramedics cut in his throat the night before. Boston police guarded the room. Second and third generation Irish-American cops. Irish on both sides of the door, Irish on both sides of the law. An Irish tradition. The fighting Irish, the killing Irish, the fucking Irish. They did this.

Aer Lingus flew the dead waiters back home to Foxford. They would be buried in the graveyard overlooking the town where my cousin Sean is buried. The national airline ships dead Irish home gratis, a custom you notice. We like the dead back home. We prefer them. We brought back Terence McSweeney and Sean Gaughan—IRA hunger strikers generations apart who pitted their bodies against the Empire.

We brought back the high-impact fascist and Radio Berlin star William Joyce to Galway. We brought back dead soldiers from the Khyber Pass, from Syria, from Byzantium, from the Western Front, from the Congo, from Lebanon.

Chopper O'Brien was with me. He drove. He got his name after shooting down a British Army helicopter, a lucky shot, but impressive still. The bullet hit the pilot under the left eye, tore a trail through his brain just as he swooped in a low lazy pattern to drop supplies at a British Army observation tower perched high on a gantry of reinforced steel straddling the border with the Irish Republic.

The helicopter jerked in the air, banked sharply and collided with the tower, scraping and shattering the blades as it fell in slow motion, the blades whirling, pieces flying free and widely as they hit the metal struts of the tower. Metal gouging metal. The co-pilot fell through an open door. Crumpled on an Irish hillside. The helicopter landed on top of him. Both pilots dead. Soon signs went up around Belfast with the decals of a helicopter against a matte-black background and a broad horizontal line through it.

Chopper and I wore sneakers, black bomber jackets, black jeans, and Armalites. We looked the part. We were dressed to kill. And that's what we were going to do.

We drove from the Banshee through the streets of South Boston, past warehouses and burnt-out buildings, past bars and people rushing through the rain to get home. It reminded me of Belfast. I tried to quiet it, the black conga of sorrow dancing around me. The rhythm of the tires against the wet road was soothing, and I looked out the window as the rain slid down the glass, trying to keep that black hood from dropping over me.

We drove around back of the Pearl Harbor Restaurant. I liked the name. Did the Americans miss the irony? You never know with Americans. I turned the car radio down. The engine was running, the windshield wipers hefting the rain away. We didn't talk. We knew what to do. We picked our rifles off the floor. We stepped out into the darkness. We pushed the doors closed. They clicked reassuringly. Heavy rain drummed off the hood.

We raised the guns as we moved inside. The chefs, waiters and rats in the kitchen looked up but didn't move or make a sound. We put our fingers up to our lips but we didn't need to. Chopper pushed the pantry doors open. We knew the table we wanted. We didn't rush. Most customers didn't notice us. People were so engrossed in talking or eating or trying to remember table manners that they don't notice what's happening around them. Chopper stayed near the salad bar. I walked over to the alcove where the Laffeys were sitting. They wouldn't be laughing for long.

Some of their bodyguards saw us. They made an effort to stand up, but halted in mid-action and then sat down again. Except for one guy. He went for a shoulder holster and I shot his hand off above the wrist. A short, sharp burst of bullets cut clean through the bone. The hand fell onto the white linen tablecloth with a thud and looked like an alien species of crab, the fingers curled up, twitching, with a thin thread of blood and sinewy material staining the starched white tablecloth. The velocity of the bullets had cauterized the artery and veins. It was good shooting. Precision. Bullet acrobatics.

By now all the Laffeys and their people were staring. Some with their backs to us had to turn around and look. I just stood there. I looked back.

"The women can go," I said. Ever merciful. I had a thing about women. About not killing them. In Belfast I stuck to this. This meant female RUC officers and some informers got away. But everyone has a weak point.

The women hesitated. I repeated it.

"The women can go over there," I said, gesturing toward the salad bar. They picked up their purses and moved away like startled cattle, their faces ashen. They looked back at their men. They looked back at me.

"Hands on the table," I said.

"What the fuck is this?" Laffey asked.

He was staring. His color was high Irish red and getting redder. An eyelid flickered.

Laffey's two brothers were watching me, trying to estimate the odds. The three bodyguards were not going to cause trouble.

"I'm here because of the Banshee."

I turned to the injured man.

"How's that hand?" I said

"It's okay."

"Jesus, how can it be okay? It's on the tablecloth."

He shrugged.

"It stings a bit, okay."

"Put it in ice," I said pointing at the basin of beers floating in the icy, slushy water. He picked up his severed hand and put it in the bucket, fingers pointing towards the ceiling.

"Good. As soon as we go, you get to a hospital."

"Okay."

"They might be able to stick it back on."

"Okay."

"If it was Belfast they could, anyway."

"Okay."

Laffey was highly agitated by now.

"What do you fucking want?"

I looked at him. He was trying to light a cigarette and fumbled the match, crumpled it up and flung it across the room.

"Why'd you attack the Banshee?" I asked.

"We didn't."

"Those morons you sent were carrying your phone number."

"So? I know everyone."

"You don't know me."

"I know you now. You're one dead fucker."

I looked at him. I thought of Belfast. I thought of the

people I'd shot. Who shot at me. Prods, RUC, squaddies. I thought of my uncle as I watched him in Ireland, thought of him in the hospital bed now. The black hood came down.

I pulled a knife from a chest scabbard and brought it in a smooth fast arc across Laffey's eyes, puncturing both eyeballs. Liquid and blood flooded out over the thin edge of the blade. His hands went up to dampen the pain. I slashed his hands. I grabbed his wrists and cut his hands off. Sheffield Steel. Nothing better. Pity it was made in England, but no situation is perfect.

I shot him in the forehead.

He fell slowly. He sat back into the seat as if he was casually leaning back to rest. I shot both his ears off. It's not as hard as it sounds. I could have cut them off with a knife, but no use going overboard.

His two brothers went for their weapons. The bodyguards decided to wait and see.

What they saw was an Armalite firing on automatic as I shot the Laffey brothers back into the deep upholstery. Another Aer Lingus trip coming up.

"Keep your hands on the table," I told the bodyguards.

They did. They were good boys.

I took their guns, cell phones and ripped the landline out of the wall. I herded the bodyguards to the back office and tied them with flexi-cuffs. I pulled the bodies from the leather sofas and across the floor into the back office. When I was done, I carried the severed hand from the ice bucket and threw it in and locked the door.

I walked back to the main dining area. I walk a lot.

I kicked a cooked chicken that had fallen off the table as hard as I could. It flew toward Chopper who tried to head it. He always wanted to play soccer for Ireland.

The sound of an approaching siren was getting louder.

"Let's go," I said.

I nodded at the women and now ex-girlfriends as we passed the salad bar. I am a vegetarian myself, but have never seen the attraction of salads. They might stay away from salad bars themselves for a while now after this.

We walked through the kitchen and out into the sharp, cold Boston night.

❧

The next day I sat beside my uncle's hospital bed. Pale blue veins in his temples pulsed faintly. Brackish fluids flecked with red leached from his body through drainage tubes. His skin was pale and covered in a sheen of sweat. I watched him as he got weaker and weaker, watched all day as the sun bled away. In the darkness, I bent down close so I could hear his breathing. I pulled a spent cartridge from my pocket and enfolded it in his hand. I told him what we did. He just lay there. Still.

I don't know if he heard me. Nurses came in at intervals, checking monitors and tubes. They looked askance at me. I stared back.

I dozed for a while. Something woke me. It was the spent cartridge hitting the cold floor, rolling away under the hospital bed. His breath rattled, once, twice, and then he stared at me, silent and unblinking.

I closed his eyes and went out into the early morning light.

Remember

I only saw him when we got up from the table in McDonogh's fish and chip shop and were standing at the counter about to pay. Jimmy was interested in one of the women behind the counter with the aim of having an encounter. I was mildly interested myself, but he saw her in the first place over plaice and chips. I could see she wasn't impressed with Jimmy so she had good taste but I thought I should let him sink or swim on his own. I turned around with my back to the counter, faced the doorway and lit up. Through the smoke I saw him.

I remembered him as being handsome, but he was now an insignificant middle-aged guy in a business suit. He had a golfing umbrella on the seat beside him and read from a glossy magazine on golf or umbrellas of the world. I hate guys who carry umbrellas at the best of times. Also, he was wearing a vest visible inside a white shirt. Strike two. What kind of women let their men go out like that? Maybe they want their men to be ridiculed outside because they've given up doing it themselves at home. Or else the women don't notice it anymore themselves.

I knew him from decades before. Thought I'd never see him again. I couldn't breathe for a few seconds and felt weak. A tremor went through me. I inhaled and started coughing. Customers looked up and so did he, but he didn't register anything out of the ordinary. Jimmy asked if I was okay and the wench behind the counter decided I was more interesting than Jimmy's fish-shit. His tipping was like his IQ, a bit on the low side and waitresses hate both.

"Let's go, for fuck sake," I said. "Flipper has more chance with her than you."

"Okay, okay, Jesus. See you soon," Jimmy turned to the waitress, but she was busy chopping the head off a big conger eel that someone had ordered. People will eat anything as long as you serve chips with it.

We walked down the aisle, Jimmy walking in front of me, and as we passed his table I pulled a straight razor from my pocket and did a drive-by slicing. I had no idea what I was going to do until it happened. It was like automatic writing, but more lethal—it happens quickly, you are in kind of a fugue state, and you operate in slow motion with fluid movements and the result is usually right. I caught him in the eye (nearest the aisle) and felt the eyeball bursting, then the grainy resistance when the blade caught his orbit bone as it passed on its trajectory back toward his ear, slicing through the cartilage. By the time we got to the door, the blade was back in my pocket. Jimmy didn't even see it because his hormone level was readjusting and he would only be able to focus on elusive mammary glands for a while.

Naturally, the victim noticed, dropped the magazine and tried to keep the eye sac fluid from draining empty. He didn't even scream. It must have been shock. I didn't look back even though I could see the bloody ear in my peripheral vision. Jimmy turned and tried to catch the eye of the waitress but the conger eel and the customer standing up with something in his eye were the only things on her menu.

We crossed the road, got into the car and Jimmy sat waiting for me to drive off. I sat there with the engine running, looking in front of me trying to decide what to do. He kept looking at me.

"What the fuck is up with you?" he said.

I glanced in the window of McDonogh's. There was a general air of mayhem. I could see about six customers on mobile phones, ringing the emergency services I presumed.

But it's hard to be sure. Maybe they were ringing other restaurants to see if they had a table, because when the chips are down people's bellies come first. I opened the car window, flicked out the cigarette and heard a siren from the emergency services. That was fast. In case the cops got curious about us, I decided to leave. Jimmy was in mid-sentence rolling a cigarette when I accelerated away from the footpath, just missing a cyclist, did a three-point turn and headed out towards Salthill. Jimmy spilled tobacco all over himself and the dashboard. He sighed and started again. Sometimes he is okay, really.

We had an apartment in Ocean Towers. Ocean, yes. Towers, no. Typical Galway hyperbole. We used it to rest up after robberies of post offices, supermarkets and armored vans. We mostly did these in England, where security is less and the cops are dense. The Gardaí knew us in Ireland, but didn't know about this place or that we were back in Galway. My home town. It was the home of Lord Haw Haw, who taunted the British from Berlin during World War II. Some kid in the Jez broke his nose in the school yard and gave him his characteristic nasal drawl. The home of Nora Barnacle, whose light enraptured James Joyce and made him carve up the English language in homage. Home of Druid Theatre, the Taibhearc, Nimmo's, Charlie Byrne's, The River God Café, Apostasy, Le Graal and the Poor Clare Convent where they had benediction on Sunday nights at 5:30. When I walked in there, the power ran through me—hurting the muscles in my legs as they spasmed from some unknown energy which the nuns seemed to bring down from heaven, leaving me weak and lightheaded for hours. Also, a lot of the Poor Clare nuns were cute.

"Will we go over the plan again for Dunnes?" Jimmy asked.

Dunne's Stores: Better Value Bleeds Them All.

"No, Jimmy. Not tonight, okay?"

"Yeah, sure."

"Do we have any white doctor coats in Mervue?" I asked.

"Yeah, I think we might okay," he said. "Want me to go and check?"

"That's sound."

In Mervue we had another house with uniforms, guns, IDs, Semtex, etcetera.

I rang the Regional Hospital, pretended I was a journalist, and asked about the victim from McDonogh's. I used an untraceable mobile phone so they couldn't track it even if it occurred to them. I was told he was in surgery and would lose the eye. Good news. I asked if there were any leads and they said they didn't know but offered to get the police to talk to me. I hung up.

I did three hundred push-ups. No sign of Jimmy yet. I heard him coming home in the early morning while I listened to the *BBC World Service*. Eventually, I fell asleep and dreamt about the dead eyes of the conger eel in McDonogh's.

Next morning I checked the living room, saw the doctor's coat, and went for a run on the Prom, a Galway institution dotted with dog shit. Ireland of the Welcomes! When I came back, I put on the coat and headed for the Regional.

I hate the smell of hospitals, so this was a big sacrifice for me. I asked for the post-op recovery room. The place was full of fucked up people and that was just the staff. I went to the third floor, found intensive care and walked in. No police. What can I say? A pale looking nurse sat at the IC monitor desk and nodded at me. I nearly winked, but managed to nod instead. Such reverence in a place like this. No talking, as if the patients surrounding us could care.

I looked down at the golfer and he looked up at me. He smiled, but I looked through him. His smile faltered. I saw the past violations, but he did not see them. I saw them with 50/50 vision, but he had zero vision and it wasn't because he had only one eye. His one eye blinked back at me, faltering a little as it tried to make internal adjustments to cope with monocular instead of binocular vision. I contemplated snipping the optical nerve of his good eye—accessing the back of the orb—it's easily done. He looked at me without any recognition.

I checked his chart. He was stable. He was going to live. Maybe.

"Remember me, fucker?" I whispered close so the nurse couldn't hear.

He looked at me again, but nothing. Selective amnesia, obviously. Maybe I could try a lobotomy. Another simple operation but you need to access the brainpan to do anything useful. I put my hand under the sheets, grabbed his balls and twisted them until his good eye was bulging and watering. I had my hand over his mouth so he couldn't shout and couldn't move.

I whispered again, "Remember me?"

"Remember offering sweets?—Do you like sweets?"

"Remember luring me to your room?—We'll just go and get some."

"Remember rubbing yourself against me?—You're so nice."

"Remember my blood pooling on the pale carpet of the room in the Great Southern?"

"Remember punching me and knocking me out?"

"Remember any of that?"

I pulled the scalpel from my coat pocket and cut into his scrotal sack. I yanked it free from the last remaining shreds of connective tissue and dropped it into a black refuse bag. Talk about spurt city. Blood sprayed everywhere. I managed to dodge it, though. The nurse jumped up. I pointed my gun at her and motioned her to sit down. She did. Nurses are conditioned to obey a direct order from a doctor, but a pistol helps as well.

The bastard was screaming now, but the ICU had good sound proofing so I wasn't too worried. When he was in mid-shout, I opened his mouth even further and stuffed in a golf ball. I took a pool cue from an inside pocket, screwed the two halves together, and smashed it down on his mouth. To hit it hard enough, I jumped off the ground to deliver maximum force.

"Fore," I shouted, but it was too late. He didn't get out of the way. I had heard the crunch of teeth. I opened his lips. Red and white splinters. A hole in one.

I cut off both ears and put them into the bag.

I chopped off his fingers and put them into the bag.

"Try playing golf now."

I was going to kill him, but thought this was better.

"What do you think?"

I tied up the nurse and left the ICU. I dropped the black bag in the incinerator chute on the way down the stairs. I wore the white coat out to the parking lot, got into the car, lit a cigarette and smiled. I rang Jimmy on the mobile. Of course, no answer.

"This is Jimmy. If you're good looking, leave me a message. Ma, if it's you, you can still leave a message."

He loved his ma.

I left a message.

"Jimmy, Dunne's is on so. I got something out of my system. Call me. I'll be at the Poor Clare's until six."

Some of those nuns were hot.

Collecting

I was talking to Billy Cameron. Billy Big Ears they called him behind his back. He could pick up radio signals from Mars. But not subliminal threats or imminent threats. It was Christmas Eve in the Irish Rover in Woodlawn. Nothing was calm. Nothing was bright. Around me Irishmen were ready to fight. It was eleven at night. It was freezing outside. A despondent Santa with a soiled outfit pushed opened the doors and stumbled in. He started singing "Silent Night."

"Silent night, holy night
All is calm, all is bright."

The crowd joined in roaring "shite" as he said bright. Everyone laughed. It was an Irish thing. Rhyming. And dying. Santa then walked around the pub with his hand out. When he reached me, I asked him to sing "Teenage Kicks." He looked at me with bloodshot eyes. They reminded me of someone. I pushed him away. He stumbled backwards trying to keep his balance.

The feigned Christmas bonhomie was suddenly gone. The crowd smelled blood. Customers shouted out requests for "The Foggy Dew," "Galway Bay," "The Irish Rover" and "She Moved Through the Fair." Complicated songs with tricky lyrical undertows which were hard to master. The crooner knew it was time to leave. As he did, the bitter wind off the Harlem River made everyone near the door flinch. Muttered fucks came from the broken-faced Irish guys who came here to drink and crave obliteration.

"You were a bit hard on him," Billy said.

I shrugged. I was asking Billy for the money he owed me

from his longstanding betting debts. Wild wagers on Gaelic football, hurling, handball, camogie—bets on all things Irish. It kept him connected to home, I suppose.

He played Gaelic football for Dublin when he was a youngster, a jackal, a Jackeen, a tall lithe warrior from Coolock with white blonde hair and the blue eyes of Ireland's Viking invaders, with the potential to be a great, who out-jumped, out-ran and out-tricked every opponent he met on the field. Unlike the sedate soccer of the Brits who ruled us for eight hundred years, Gaelic football is a potent mix of bone-crunching tackles, elbows in the face, balletic fielding of high balls, loping solo runs and shots at goal that have murderous velocity.

Billy started betting in Claude's Casino as a kid. Nothing serious. Then it got serious. He began to miss football practice. First deadly sin. He began to miss easy goals, which was more deadly. The crowd booed him. He started drinking. He was cut from the team. He burned down the clubhouse and then he concentrated on Claude's full time. He was there in the morning before they opened. The staff made sure they opened on time or he would cause trouble. At closing time, he was the last to leave. He sent letters to the local newspapers asking for twenty-four hour opening. He escaped Ireland for owing thousands of Euros and being a person of interest in multiple suspected arson attacks.

I didn't care about any of that. Live and let live is my motto, except for amateur Santa Clauses that might be carrying TB, fleas, lice, etcetera, and who reminded me of someone. And except for anyone that owes me money. Billy was weeks overdue. He was married to Lucinda Craven, daughter of the Dublin Football Team coach. Billy thought he was paying him back from being dropped by stealing his daughter, but it was the other way around. Lucinda could have been called Lucifer. Her father was delighted to get rid of her. Billy didn't see it coming. As usual. They now lived happily never after in the Irish enclave of Woodlawn in the north Bronx. They had five kids. I felt sorry for the kids. They all had Billy's ears for a start.

Collecting this money was a point of honor. I never missed appointments, dates, deadlines or dead-lines. It was Christmas, but I didn't believe in the Jesus racket, Bethlehem, the manger, the shepherds, the wise men, the rising from the dead (I know that's Easter, okay?) so for me it had no resonance.

Billy fobbed me off.

"I'll have it in the New Year. Sure. You know well I am good for it."

"I don't know that," I said.

He looked at me. It wasn't the usual Irish way of doing business. He expected me to say sure, I know you're good for it. Sure, it's Christmas. Sure, no problem. Sure, the New Year is fine. Sure—run off home and pray for us all.

"Sure, fuck that," I said.

"Where's your soft side?"

I didn't answer. I looked at my reflection in the ceiling-high mirror behind the bar, saw Billy in profile.

He put down the whiskey.

"Ah, fuck off," he said in that ambiguous Irish way that can be taken any way. I took it the wrong way.

"I want it now, tonight."

"I'll see you right in the New Year."

"Fuck the New Year."

"What?"

"Fuck the New Year—are you deaf?"

"Take it easy."

Customers were looking over at us.

"Don't tell me to take it easy."

"What are you going to do—shoot me?"

I said nothing.

"It's not that much."

"That's true," I said. "That's not the point."

"What's the point?"

102

"It's the principle."

"What principle?"

"The paying what you fucking owe principle. Paying the principal principle. Paying the fucking interest principle. You ever hear of that?"

"I don't owe that much."

"I know. We did this part already."

"I swear I'll have it in the New Year. I don't have it now. You know, presents and all for the kids."

"Are you going to pluck turkeys or something to get the money together?"

"Turkeys, me arse. I have money coming from home."

I found that hard to believe.

He put his hand on my shoulder.

"We're all Irish aren't we? We have to stick together."

I shook his hand free.

"Have that money first of January."

He laughed.

"You're a dark one," he said. He winked, drained the hot whiskey, put down the glass and headed out into the night. I saw Billy's sallow skin pucker around his tired eyes as he left, giving me a friendly wave and forced smile.

I turned back to my own drink.

It was bothering me. I felt I was too easy on him. There was weakness reflected in my own hesitation. I listened to "Jump Around" by House of Pain blasting from the jukebox. It eased me a little.

⍦

At midnight, I left the Irish Rover. I was slightly drunk but could probably drive no problem. An Irish skill. Or so we thought. Until we careened into abutments and over guard rails into canals and rivers and lakes and flamed into predatory trees on the side of lonesome country roads. The frost was caked on the bonnet and windscreen. I got into the car, pulling the revolver from my waistband and dropping it on the floorboard. I turned the heater on to melt the ice.

I put on "Dirty Old Town" by The Pogues and tried to remember what it was like before I came to this dirty old town, before I came to the Bronx, before I settled for collecting debts, helping keep the peace in Woodlawn.

I should never have left Ireland. I wouldn't except for a major robbery foul up. We ran into the AIB in Tuam and John Dolan tripped on the uneven, original sixteenth-century flagstones. He blew the heads off three money serfs by accident. It was on full automatic. It was a trick shot, really. The flagstones were a tourist attraction, but now the bank had an extra but macabre attraction which the West of Ireland Tourist Board would not promote. I shot Dolan on the spot because he was careless and didn't have great poise. I did. I caught his Armalite on his way down and slung it over my shoulder. We got the money and then the boat out of Ireland to France, then Spain and then Canada. Now I was in the Arctic circle of Woodlawn and the Bronx wasting my time trying to get my edge back, trying to forget those three civilians with their shattered brains and faces lying in pools of dark black blood on the bank floor. I didn't care about John Dolan. He had it coming.

Billy Cameron had it coming as well if he didn't pay up. I didn't know why I gave him an extra week. He wanted to buy presents for his wife and kids. He wanted to go home and put his kids to bed. He wanted to decorate the tree. But maybe he wanted to get away with it, to keep the money for another week, to abuse my good nature. I could not get rid of the deep-seated irritant that was Billy Cameron. I didn't like him. He reminded me of my father.

A bull-shitter, a big man, a blow hard, a bully, a broken down bastard, a big baby who struggled mightily when I held him down, held his head under, watched his eyes bulge distorted through the water, bloodshot eyes, blood beginning to seep from his nostrils. I let him up and he coughed, vomited bath water, aromatic bubble-bath sprayed the floor when he caught his breath and looked at me, words tumbling from his pale puckered lips, what have I done what have I done.

He knew well.

"You know well."

"What?"

"You. Know. Fuck. Ing. Well."

I hit his head against the ceramic bath on each of syllable. Blood ran down from his scalp, mingling in the water.

"You. Know. Right. Well. Daddy. Io." (seven blows) "Have you water in your ears or something?"

He saw it in my eyes, the far long look that never lies. I pushed his head under water again. He tried to fight back. He squirmed, he flayed, I slayed him. Me, the newborn king.

"Fairy Tale of New York" was on by the time the ice melted enough for me to see through a narrow slit. I hit the wipers and they began to eat away at the edges of ice. I put the car in drive and eased out of the parking space. The roads were dry. There was no banked snow. It was easy. I drove home to McLean Avenue, Irish bars and Irish tricolors hanging from neat houses where the exiled Irish try to mold a middle class life for themselves. I had a basement apartment in a family house. Sometimes I could hear children playing upstairs and it soothed me. Sometimes I was invited for Sunday dinner but made my excuses and eventually they stopped asking. I never caused trouble. I never invited small talk. I never mingled. I always paid rent on time. (Billy Cameron, take note.) I hovered on the periphery of melancholia and austerity. I did sit ups until my muscles ached. I did push-ups until my sweat hit the floor like drops of rain that fall without warning on dry Irish country roads in the middle of the summer.

I sat in my armchair reading Flannery O'Connor. Her name sounded Irish. Her gothic Southern outlook fitted my own. Billy Cameron kept intruding. I wanted to make sure that fucker knew I meant business. I was going to outline the situation for him. I looked at the clock. Three in the morning. Fuck.

I threw the book across the room. I grabbed the revolver from the floor. I went outside into the freezing wind, slamming the door behind me. I de-iced the car again. Jesus, would this weather ever break? I sat there in the pale moonlight waiting for the ice to flake away, the radio playing Black 47, my mind picking at the scab that was Billy Cameron. I drove to a payphone picked at random. Some Irish Eskimos were still out, staggering, lighting cigarettes, reeling home. I rang the house. Lucifer answered.

"Is Billy there?"

"Do you know what fucking time it is?"

"3:31, if I'm not mistaken."

"Billy is that you, you fucking eejit? If that's you, you're a fucking dead man."

"No it's not Billy Big Ears. Get him."

"Who the fuck is this?" She had a great grasp of cursing, like all the Irish.

"Is he there? I just need to talk to him for a minute. It'll be over there in a minute unless you shut up for a minute. I'll be over there in a minute if you don't answer my question."

"Fuck. Hang on."

I could hear Billy's name being hollered over the line.

"No, he's not here so fuck off."

She hung up.

❧

I drove around to their house. Billy's car was not there. I drove around Woodlawn until I found his car in the lot behind Keenan's Bar. I checked the car first in case he was frozen to death in the driver's seat. No such luck. I walked through the kitchen entrance and saw him at the counter with some cronies from Dublin. I went outside and sat in my car with the engine running and played Sinead O'Connor's sad keening. At five, I saw him stagger outside alone. I eased out of my car and quickly walked up on his blind side. He swayed beside his car. He fumbled with his keys. When he got in, I got in the passenger side. He didn't even know I was sitting there until he had his own door closed. He jumped in his seat, which isn't easy.

"Jesus, you fucking scared the bollicks out of me."

"You're lucky you still have any."

"What?"

"You. Are. Luck. Y. You. Still. Have. Them." (eight blows off the dashboard)

Blood cascaded out of his nose. He held it with his hands. He moaned. He turned back to me.

"God I'm bleeding all over."

"Not all over yet. Billy, I want that fucking money now."

"I thought we agreed."

"Yes, that's before you fucked off to another bar and drank for the last four hours. What happened to the wife and children, the crib sob story scenario?"

"What?"

"The wife, the kids huddling around the Christmas tree, fairy lights. That scenario."

"I thought you didn't believe in Christmas."

"Who said that?"

"Don't know, heard it somewhere. Anyways, it's okay to have a drink, sure, at Christmastime, isn't it?"

I was shaking and it wasn't from the cold.

I took out the revolver and pushed it to his temple. I fired. He was in the middle of another peroration but I had reached my limit. Nothing would have saved him, even Jesus. The noise was enormous. Blood spattered the windscreen, the roof was pock-marked with clots of blood and brain tissue, the exit wound severed an artery because blood cascaded around the car like a faulty water sprinkler as he fell forward onto the dashboard.

I was drenched. I was deaf. I was raging. But it was fading. The razor blade scratching at my eye socket feeling that had been building all night since I let him walk away was dissipating. I would know in the future not to extend credit.

I checked his wallet. Eighteen hundred dollars. The fucking eejit only owed twelve hundred. I threw six hundred on his body. I have principles. The cops would take it probably and buy drinks. I didn't want to spoil everyone's Christmas. I smashed the courtesy light with the butt of the revolver and opened the door, looked around, all was peaceful, all was quiet. That reminded me of something but I couldn't place it.

I kept low until I got to my car. I started it up and left the parking lot slowly, without any drama. I had enough for one night. I looked in the mirror. I was covered in gore and blood. I hoped Billy was happy now.

Because I was.

Sure

Sixth day following the van.
Using up fuel, time, patience.
Smoking.
Car full of acrid blue smoke.
Tainting my lungs.
I had places to be. People to see. Cousins to visit. Banks to stake out. Guys to lay out. Dead. For money. For insults. For friends.
Time is money. This is America.
Where the hell is that armored truck going? Can't anyone follow a pattern? Do you know how much extra work this is? Do you know what this is doing to my blood pressure? Not to mention my lungs? I can feel the smoke from Victor's cigarette impregnating the capillaries, destroying my baby-face skin. And it's penetrating the fabric of the car seats. And it's curling into the barrel of the guns lying on the floor mat.
It's not surprising that we often get riled up by the time we pull off a job. Sometimes we just have to do something even if it's not ideal, even if it's half-arsed and doesn't make sense or is suicidal or impossible or next to impossible. Just to release the adrenalin dam so we don't explode or start smashing up someone's automobile.
Or apartment.
Or super.
Or drinking buddy.
Or random strangers.
Or police.

Or traffic wardens.

Or preppy students.

Or Wall Street types with smug faces.

Or just start firing shots at random out the window.

The black-gray eyes of Victor were watching me.

"You sure?" he asked.

"Yeah, sure."

Sure I'm sure.

Sure. Sure.

"Dead sure," I added.

I pulled out from the armored van's wake and sped by in the passing lane. We would try again tomorrow. I watched it disappear in my rearview mirror.

ॐ

Last Friday I was driving upstate on the way to Ossining to visit my cousin Leo Temple who was serving fifteen to life for being in the wrong place at the wrong time, i.e. Chase Bank foyer with an unapproved withdrawal slip, a pistol. He probably lost patience and had to act (see above). I might be bad but he is terrible. He has no self-control. I'm surprised he lasted so long without being caught. He had great luck up to that. Plus, he is very calm once the job starts. You have to give him credit for that. He was robbing since he was fourteen. Bicycles, foals, turf, Post Offices, cars, pubs, cafes, take outs, rifles, paintings, jewelry, live turkeys, slabs of ham and dead lamb. An eclectic mix.

Anyway, I noticed a blue and white GARDA security van in the slow lane, the chassis riding low. The sluggish speed confirmed a heavy load.

I wasn't speeding, otherwise I would have missed it. I was just cruising, letting the long miles soothe me, letting the rhythmic sigh of wheels against tarmac lull me. In Ireland, you could speed day and night on the wrong side of the road with no lights on—with no tax, no insurance, with bald tires, with no seat belt, with stolen safes in the back-seat, with warm bodies tied up on the floor. The chance of seeing the Gardaí was minimal. But here I was on an expired visitor's visa, so no point asking for trouble by bombing up and down the beautiful smooth blacktop of New York state.

I noticed the name of the GARDA van straight off because it is close to the spelling of the Gardaí. I thought it was a good omen. Also, I was interested in armored security vans in general. We had done a few in Ireland. No police protection. Armored vans blithely wandering the Irish countryside. They asked for it.

On those armored van jobs in Ireland, we never hurt anyone except the reputation of the security managers, the police, the government, the Special Branch, the Gardaí, the banks, and the security van companies. In the end, security details were increased so much that it was time to drop them. They had Irish Army rangers escorts, costing thousands of euros of taxpayers money. The Government would not even ask the banks to pay. They deserved to be robbed just for that.

Then we started on ATM machines encased in the feeble walls of small supermarkets all over the country which we easily pulled asunder with stolen backhoes from neighboring building sites. €100,000 every time. So easy. It became boring even. It was fun driving down country roads with heavy cash dispensers weighing us down. Backhoes were then outlawed. Now that's overreaction. Hard to clear a building site without them. Need an army of conscripts to do that. Then we used dynamite and Semtex. They were outlawed already, so we were ahead on that one. Then they banned most outlying towns from having ATM machines. Then they reduced the amount in each ATM.

Then we moved to bank cash distribution centers. A puny façade of gates, guards, barriers and time locks. They were nearly all built backed onto marsh or scrubland. The designers must have looked at the mud-filled land and felt confident. The Nazis got mired down by mud, rain and snow going into Russia so we should be okay, they thought.

111

Typical Irish magical thinking. You have to think laterally. That's what we did. We timed when police and army escorts dropped off the cash. We noticed they always left as soon as the outer gates of the money centers were closed, before the money made it into the secure area. The police and army headed off for their tea break and the cash-fat armored vans sat around in the courtyard for hours before they were brought into the latest in high-tech secure vaults.

On a June Bank Holiday, we drove two Range Rovers taken a week earlier from the leafy suburbs of Dublin to the isolated back roads abutting the marshy land that stretched for fifty yards behind the cash compound. We roped makeshift rafts to the roof racks for the waterlogged sections. We watched a van carrying an estimated €8 million enter the depot. We watched the long convoy of Gardaí and army vehicles speeding home for their supper.

We drove straight at the security fence bordering the soggy land which we had cut earlier but left in situ, held together by fishing line and duct tape. The two Range Rovers crashed through the fence, slogging across the muddy ground until we reached the waterlogged sections, threw down the rafts, drove across the pontoon and crashed through the next token fence, piled out, eight of us with Armalites, masks and adrenaline overdoses, filled the Range Rovers with €10 million, two million more than we expected (we couldn't have carried anymore anyway) and drove out the front gates and away. The guys in the secure vault section could only watch us on CCTV. They couldn't contact the police via the landlines they were using—so amateurish. We had disabled them as soon as we jumped out of the Range Rovers. It was clockwork. It was poetry in motion. It was foresight by us. It was poor insight by the Gardaí. Again.

❧

As I tailed the GARDA van, I kept well back in case they had a keyhole camera flush with the metal surface scanning traffic. I couldn't see one, but it could still be there. I used Zeiss binoculars that I brought from Belfast to scan the chassis, the windows, the tires. I scanned the paint to determine general quality. It looked pristine. It would be a tough assignment. I wasn't interested, though, just professionally curious. I had tons of money from the Irish jobs. I was about to speed up and overtake them when I noticed the armored van slow. I maintained position and observed.

It began to coast into a service area. Maybe a pick-up. Maybe not. I followed and it joined the McColon's drive-thru queue. I stayed two cars behind. The van stopped by the order station and then proceeded to pick up. I flung my burger out the window as soon as the van joined the traffic again. That crap was a killer.

I couldn't believe it. Just when you thought you saw everything, something like this restored your belief in human stupidity. I followed the van for ten miles noting pick-ups. Scanned the chassis more closely. Overtook the van and watched the windows. No smoked glass. Petty way to cut costs. Once you can see in, you are halfway there. You can ID the guys then no problem. Elementary mistake. I could see the driver and co-driver eating fries and burgers. Two fat scoffers. Click. Click. Click.

I would be skipping the Sing Sing visit to Leo that day. I watched the van trundling along on an uphill section. Six wide lanes over. The blue and white box. The happy steal. Asking for it. I smiled. I smirked. I cracked up. I inhaled. My cousin Leo would understand. He would love it.

Then I called Victor, a friend from Belfast. Told him I wanted to see him. The usual place. Parked the car in Woodlawn. Took the 4 train downtown. Read a Parker novel, *The Score*, and ignored everyone around me. Saw a few Irish guys I knew. Gave them imperceptible nods. The Galway salute. Stark wrote like a criminal. It was authentic accounts of heists and scams and jobs. The only one to match his was Ed Bunker and he was the real thug thing.

Told Victor the van story. Stopping for burger and fries.

He smiled. He coughed. He laughed. He grimaced. Big tears crept down his face. I sat back. I was smug. I was elated. I was floating. I was back. I could feel it.

"Are you sure?" he said.

"Sure I'm sure."

❧

Seventh day started gray and dreary. Black rain clouds massed over New York. Rain spilled down in unrelenting sheets. The Hudson was pockmarked with heavy drops flung across the surface. Commuters scurried along the pavement avoiding the water running from the gutters. I picked Victor up from his apartment on McLean Avenue in Woodlawn. He lived with an American woman who loved his accent. He wasn't Mister Romanticism, though. When he proposed to her, he left the ring on the table in its box and said "There is something over there for ya." When she screamed and said "Are we engaged?" he said "You never know." He is a bit understated.

"Better luck today," he said.

I nodded. Rain always brought me luck. It was easier to distract people. Cops got slowed down. It cleans the streets. It clears my head. Negative ions-like.

We picked up the GARDA van at its depot. We had to drive by a few times to catch it exiting. I watched the drivers. It wasn't easy. The wipers were on max. It was the same drivers as the Friday of the McColon stop. I felt elated.

"It's them."

"Are you sure?"

"Sure I'm sure."

We followed as it did pick-ups. When it neared the McColon service area where it stopped the previous Friday, I tensed. It turned in. I said "We're on."

Victor said "You were right."

"You're right I'm right."

The rain was falling even heavier now.

"Jesus, we will need Wellingtons at this rate," he said.

We could see fuck all. The blue and white GARDA van eased into the ordering lane.

Victor looked over at me and flexed his firing finger a few times. He picked up his Armalite. Once the van made the order, we sped around against traffic to the pick-up area with cars blowing their horns at us. It was rainy. It was messy. Visibility was nearly zero. The guys in the van could order without getting out because of a speaker device like the cops use on cop cars. "Move along there, dopey." It was a miracle no one had captured these buffoons ordering fries and burgers on YouTube.

As the van stopped to pick up the order, I got out of the car, pulled the balaclava down and sprinted crouching to sneak up on the driver's side. They had to open the door to pick up the food—no hatches in the front. Once the door opened a fraction of an inch, that was enough. As the driver leaned down to pick up the happy meal, I rushed over and yanked on his arm so his face hit the door frame. I aimed over his head at the shotgun guy. I shot him through his smartly creased blue and white uniform. I shot the fat driver as gravity pulled him past me onto the wet pavement. His head exploded in a crimson blowback.

I scrambled in, pushed the neatly uniformed dead shotgun guy out of the way and placed a Semtex charge against the bulwark of the money storage unit. Used just enough to blow the panel in. The interior panels are always fragile—they don't expect people to be breaking in from inside the van. No guards in there. I knew because they only ordered two happy meals. Cutbacks, I suppose. I jumped outside while the charge detonated. Clambered into the money pit. The bags were heavy. I threw them up front. I glanced in at McColon's. I could see Victor standing on the counter waving the rifle and sipping a soft drink through a straw. I didn't touch the coin bags.

I checked the watch. Two minutes gone—time to go. I got up front and threw the bags onto the wet courtyard, greasy from rain, gas droplets, fries and blood. Some of the bags bounced off the fat driver.

"Sorry about that, Mister," I said.

Inside the balaclava, the sweat ran into my eyes. I flung the bags into the car, its doors still open, the engine still running, the rain still falling, Victor still grandstanding. It was risky with just two. But he was the perfect villain. And I don't like sharing with too many. And the rain made it perfect. A car idling with flashers on in this rain is no problem.

Victor was watching me. When he saw I was almost done he fired a burst into the ceiling. I could see it but not hear it. I saw chips of tiling fall from the ceiling and heads ducking. He leaped from the counter. He came strolling out. He helped me pick up the remaining bags. Two minutes, fifty seconds. I could hear sirens. The rain would delay them. And confuse them. Although that was easy.

I reversed, hit the gas and sped from the service area onto I-87. Victor handed me a happy meal. I flung it out the window. I was a vegetarian.

"That shit will kill you, Victor," I said.

"Are you sure?"

"Yeah. I'm sure."

No Exceptions

We saw him going into Cannon's.

And maybe that's what we'd have to use to grab him.

"Okay. Go and bring him out," Pender said.

He looked around at us.

"The place is crawling with Brits as well, so watch it."

Pender and the driver waited in the car. Me and Jack checked our guns and the street and got out. When we reached the security cage, we were inspected through close-circuit cameras. We were asked who we were.

"The IRA, who else?" I said. "Open the fucking door. It's pissing sleet out here."

It was freezing. Cold, slanting rain was coming down from the Belfast Hills.

"Jesus, will you shut up," Jack admonished me and then gave his name, where he was from, his temperature, who he knew, etcetera, so eventually the electronic door mechanism clicked open and we walked in.

We weren't the most active active-service-unit in Belfast, so maybe the doorman had a point to be cautious. I like to think I am evenhanded.

"Hello lads," the doorman said. "Sorry about that, but we have to be careful."

"No problem," Jack said.

"Fuck you," I said. I'm a bit fickle I suppose.

He looked at me but said nothing. I shook the rain from my jacket at him.

As we passed, he stood back further but I nodded in his

direction to illustrate my anger management skills. I was not a total dick. Or maybe I was. Anyway, you never know when one of these guys might take offence and dial 1-800-TOUT TALK.

The place was packed and full of sound, the thump of music. I spotted Sean. When I saw Jack look in my direction I nodded toward the back bar.

We got through the crowd. Jack tapped Sean on the shoulder and I watched his reaction. The hand holding the pint faltered slightly and I saw his pupils dilate but he recovered quickly and brought the glass to his lips. I was impressed.

"Hello lads," he said. "Can I buy ye a pint?"

Jack took charge.

"No. We need to go now. Pender wants to see you."

I thought his hand faltered once again but he nodded and said "Okay. Be with you in a few minutes, just going to finish this. No use wasting good drink."

"Quit the shit," Jack said. "We gotta go, now. Put the fucking pint down and let's go."

"Take it easy, Jack," I said, putting my hand on his arm. "This place is too busy to be pulling guns out."

"Smart boy you got there. He'll go far I'd say. Far, far."

He was right.

Jack was furious.

"Okay. Hurry the fuck up, so."

I looked around. The dance floor was full. Lean boys with shaved heads danced the pogo, jumping in high waves to the jagged staccato rhythms of the Undertones, Stiff Little Fingers and the Outcasts. A sea of modern Maasai warriors.

"Right, lads. I'm finished. Lead on, McDuff."

"What's this McDuff shit?" Jack asked and Sean winked at me.

"Not a literary chap then, are we?" Sean said.

He looked at me again but I stared back. His smile dissolved and his eyes became fearful. I smiled, leaned in close to him and whispered.

"Don't do that again."

Jack, puzzled, looked in our direction but said nothing. As we left, I felt great. I felt alive.

We left Cannon's through the back entrance, walked around to the front, surveyed the road and crossed to the car with Sean between us. Jack got in followed by Sean and then me.

"Where the fuck were you?" Pender said. "Jesus, I thought I was going to have to go in there. A fucking Brit patrol just passed as well. What were you fucking doing?"

Clearly, he had a favorite word.

"We were watching the crowd do the pogo," I said. "You know how it is,"

"What the fuck are you talking about?"

"The pogo—like the Maasai—like dark chappies from Africaland."

"Jesus, I'm getting too old for this crap."

"Should we go?" the driver asked.

"Of course we should fucking go. Is this your driving test or something? Jesus, I'm surrounded by morons."

The driver looked at me in the rearview mirror. I nodded at him and felt the tension lift. We joined the heavy slow traffic down the Falls road and headed out of Belfast. Nobody spoke.

I loved Belfast the first day I arrived there. The Belfast Hills overlooked the City giving a sense of protection and permanence, which was an illusion. Down in the City were the killing machines. Heavy rain rolled in from the sea. It was like Galway again. I love rain and the wet, slick roads. Hedgerows dripping with rain. Mist evaporating from roadways after sudden summer showers.

When I say this to people they don't know what I'm talking about.

I liked the Belfast accents, the sense of black humor. Of course the City was full of violence, chaos, pain and suffering as well. I also liked these qualities and felt at ease there.

When I say this to people they do not know what I am talking about either.

Most people don't know what I am talking about.

As we drove south it grew darker and colder and we drove through mist followed closely by persistent, heavy rain.

"Jesus, this weather is shite," Pender said.

"I kind of like it," I said.

"You would."

He turned around to look at me.

"You worry me sometimes, you know?"

And then he turned back in his seat.

I spotted the driver looking at me in the mirror again. His blue-green eyes looked away. I watched the lights of isolated farmhouses, thinking about the work before us. The low volume of the car radio invoked a meditative state. Johnny Cash was singing "Wanted Man."

"Can I have a fag?" Sean asked beside me.

"No you can't have a fucking fag. This isn't a fucking school tour."

"Jesus, take it easy. He only wants a fag," I said.

Pender looked around at me again.

"What's your fucking problem? You are not in charge yet, you know."

"Yet," I said, and stared back at him. After a while, he turned around, sighing.

"Okay, okay. Give him a fag."

I lit a cigarette and handed it to Sean.

"This doesn't mean I love you, you know, but I might hold your hand later when the going gets tough."

"Jesus, knock that shit off will you, McGowan? You're fucking sick."

I smiled and watched the passing darkness.

"Where are we going anyway?" asked Sean after the cigarette was finished. "I don't recognize this road."

"Just mind your own fucking business," Pender said at the wet windshield in front of him. "It's on a need-to-know basis and you know too much already. That's why we're all going on this little spin. You'll find out soon in any case, okay? Almost there."

"That's the turn there," the driver said.

He slowed, checked the mirror and drove down a narrow laneway bounded by high hedges. We stopped at a two-story farmhouse and Pender took charge again.

"Okay, it looks clear. Drive around, park and hide the car. Keep watch at the bottom of the road. Use the radio and the Armalite, in that order, if you have to."

"What password will we use?" the driver asked. His nickname was Crip because that's how you ended up if you crossed him. "How about Crip Space?" he suggested.

I laughed.

"No" Pender said.

"What about Crips ?"

He always wanted to live in LA.

Pender sighed.

"Use pogo," I said, settling things.

"Okay," Pender said. "Anything for a quiet life. Let's go."

"Right, Sean. Move it." I said.

We opened the back door. Jack and I went to check the rooms while Pender stood just inside the door holding Sean's arm. We should have checked before they came in but I knew it was safe already because I have psychic ability, which didn't really fit with my current lifestyle. No mantras, meditation or vegetarian sausages for me. I didn't believe in killing dumb animals except for informers and loyalist gunmen.

"Okay, it's safe."

"Right. In you go, Sean," I said.

We got to the bedroom, which had the best noise-proofing, and I put a gun to Sean's head.

"Okay, strip off."

121

"Look there's no need for this. I'll tell you anything you want," Sean said.

"Don't worry, I know you will. Just like you did with the Brits," I said. "Now take your clothes off or I'll do it for you."

"McGowan, I'm still in charge here so watch it," Pender said, staring at me.

I smiled and shrugged.

"Okay, you strip him. I won't be jealous."

"Jesus, I'm getting you fucking transferred ASAP."

Sean stripped to his underwear. He was wearing boxer shorts with Mickey Mouse on them. I expected a Tricolor or a Sinn Fein slogan. I thought it was strange gear to be wearing. So American. So banal. We bound his hands and feet with flexi-cuffs. We seated him at a table. I stood behind him. Jack stood at the door.

"These cigarettes might come in handy, especially if placed on the genitalia while lit," I said in an Oxbridge accent, throwing them onto the table.

Pender got up, pulled his revolver and pointed it at my face. I watched the bullets in the chamber and the dark hole of the barrel.

"Keep the fuck out of this!" he roared at me.

"Okay, okay. Only trying to help."

Pender sat down and started the interrogation by hitting Sean across the forehead with his handgun. Impressive. It had to hurt.

"Right," Pender said and straightened. "This is a duly constituted court martial conducted by Óglaigh na hÉireann. You are charged with treason. How do you plead?"

"Fuck this. I haven't done anything."

At least he had spirit.

"Do you agree that you're a member of the IRA?"

"Yes, of course I'm a fucking member."

I wondered if the two of them were related, linguistically-wise.

"Okay, since you are, then you recognize the legitimacy of a duly appointed court martial, correct?"

"Okay, okay, yes."

"This is the court martial summons. Want to read it, Sean?"

"No, Pender. It's all bullshit."

"Okay. Do you plead guilty to charges of being a police informer, yes or no?"

"No. No fucking way. Not fucking guilty. Fuck off."

"That's a not guilty then," I said into his ear. He must have forgotten I was there because he jumped out of the seat, but because his legs were tied he struck his head on the side of the table as he fell over.

"McGowan, keep the fuck out of this or there'll be another execution," Pender said, watching Sean make his way back into his seat.

"Isn't that a bit premature?" I said. "Don't you mean court martial? What about being innocent until proven dead?"

"Look, I'm warning you. Shut the fuck up until I ask you to do something," Pender replied. "I've done this before. It's bad enough without a psycho like you making things worse."

"Jesus, take it easy. I'll behave myself."

"Okay, where the fuck was I?" Right. We enter a plea of not guilty. If guilty, the sentence is execution. You know that?"

"Yeah, I know," Sean muttered.

"For the past six months there's been raids on arms dumps and safe houses and interception of active service units. RPGs were taken as well as Armalites, Semtex and ammunition."

Pender paused.

"One of our people in the RUC established there was a high-ranking IRA member feeding information to the RUC. We thought it might be you from the physical description, but most of the rest didn't fit. Anyway, nobody could believe it except that psychic psycho standing behind you. That's why he's here."

He finished by pointing toward me.

"That's a load of bullshit. Jesus, I was worried there for a minute."

"Why's that, I wonder," I said into his ear like an act of contrition. He jumped again, startled, but I caught him this time.

Pender got up from the table, picked up the gun and pointed it at me.

"McGowan, this is the last time I'm warning you."

I looked at him for a while and sat down.

"The next time you raise that gun against me you better use it," I said.

Pender sat down. He was breathing heavily and sweating. He dropped his gun on the table and looked around him in a daze. A blood vessel at his temple pulsed wildly. Jack was looking back and forth between us. The tension in the room was high.

Pender refocused and restarted the interrogation.

"It's looking real bad for you, Sean. We've got strong evidence."

"Like what? It's bullshit, anyway. What did that faggot behind me ever do for the cause?"

I jumped up, pulled a stiletto from an ankle scabbard and stabbed him through the shoulder blade. He screamed and struggled to get away but fell backward over the chair onto the floor. Not much blood, but amazing pain. Pender looked at me but didn't move.

"That was personal," I said. "Sorry for the wee interruption."

Pender looked at me a long time and then looked away.

"Lift him up, will you?" he asked Jack.

Jack moved away from the door and picked up Sean. He was now sweating, had difficulty breathing and was pale. I pulled the stiletto free. He fainted for a while.

"How the fuck is he supposed to answer questions semiconscious?" Pender asked.

"I thought he was supposed to be a brave IRA volunteer," I said. "What's the problem? We needed some action anyway. I was getting bored. He's a big mouth, as if we didn't know. This is taking forever."

"If you'd keep your mouth shut and your hands to yourself we might get someplace," Pender said.

I shrugged and wiped the blood from the blade on Sean's Mickey Mouse shorts.

Pender sighed and addressed Sean again when he recovered consciousness.

"Look, we know that evidence from the RUC mole is dicey but we leaked some information about a safe house and only told you and the next day the Brits raided it so basically you're fucked."

"I don't care. It wasn't me. It could be anyone. It could be fucking chance."

"No way," I said.

Pender didn't even look at me.

"Look, we leaked something else to you as well and two days later an arms dump was raided. There was fuck-all there, as you probably heard, since you get paid by the quality of the info."

"I didn't tell anyone anything."

"Pogo, come in," the walkie-talkie crackled.

Everyone jumped, even me. Tension city. We grabbed our pistols. I taped Sean's mouth. Pender had the radio.

"Crip, what's happening?"

"You have to say over, over" came the tinny reply.

"Crip what the fuck is happening—fuck you over."

"Brits really close. Looks like a random patrol though, maybe four squaddies. No back up or helicopters. Over."

"Okay, we'll stay put for a while, tell us what's happening, over."

"They're just approaching the turn off now so we'll know soon. I think I see another four guys further back.

Over."

"Fuck okay over." Pender looked at me then Jack. "If we're caught with a prisoner it's bad. But if we're caught with a dead prisoner, we're fucked. So everyone fucking relax."

"First four have passed," the walkie-talkie crackled. "Looks good. Over."

"Right, what about the others?" Pender said.

"You have to say over," I said.

"Fuck, Crip, what about the others? Fuck you over."

We waited. I was relaxed again. I accept what happens no matter what it is. This is a good philosophy of life. Nothing will ever bother you then. You feel safe because it is your fate. I should have been a philosopher, really. Sean was frightened.

"Rest of foot patrol has passed. Looks okay. Over."

"Great, keep under observation in case they double back, over."

"Right. Over."

We waited ten minutes. Then it was time. I untied Sean's legs and pulled the tape off his mouth.

"Kneel down, Sean," I said.

"Jesus, lads, you can't be serious. You know I wouldn't say anything to the Brits. Look, I was shot by a Para and you know I killed all around me in the early days."

"Kneel down, Sean."

"Jesus, lads, for fuck's sake this can't be right. You know I hate touts. I'd kill myself if I was one. I wouldn't even wait for you to come looking for me. There is no way I did this. It doesn't make sense."

"Sean, kneel down. It's time," I said.

"Look, please. I'm on my knees now, is that what you want? Will that make you happy? Please don't do this to me, okay? Anything I said to them was just bullshit—it was all crap stuff, you know."

"Is that a fact?" I said.

"I didn't want to go back into the cages. It nearly killed me last time. I did plenty for the cause over the years. Remember that machine gun attack near Gough Barracks? I killed three Brits on my own, you fuckers. This is nothing. You got to let me go."

"Let me think," Pender said.

"Don't bother. You might get an embolism," I said.

"I'm in charge here. I might refer it back."

"Refer it back me arse. Nothing gets referred back, Pender. Do you think this is a fucking election recount or something?"

"It sounds harmless enough," Pender said.

"Nothing is harmless except a body."

Pender was sweating.

"No exceptions," I said.

I quickly pulled a black hood over Sean's head, stepped back and fired two shots.

It was loud.

Before the reverberations of the gunfire finished, I said to Jack "Okay, let's wrap this fucker up and get out of here."

Pender roared at me that we hadn't passed sentence, that the execution was illegal.

"So? What were you going to do?"

"I'm the commanding officer, McGowan. As soon as we get back, I'm reporting you."

I raised the pistol slowly and he looked at me with a mixture of disbelief and recognition and made a halfhearted effort to go for his gun.

"Report this back, why don't you?"

I shot him in the heart, the throat and the forehead and that was that.

"Well, Pender," I said, standing over his body. "You're not in charge anymore."

Jack stood there looking at me.

"Let's go. Two fuckers for the price of one. He was ready to crack," I said to Jack.

I know it rhymes.

Jack pulled the polythene sheet to the center of the room and dragged both bodies across the rough concrete floor. I picked up my cigarettes from the table and went outside. The night air smelled good and the stars were clear in the December sky.

I lit a cigarette and did the pogo.

And that was that.

My Beautiful, Brash, Beastly Belfast

A Saracen parked askew, silhouetted at dusk against the fog rising slowly off the Lagan, the high rimmed wheels straddling the fractured footpath, the dented gray metal armor a dull sheen in the fading light.

The boy runs across the stone littered road toward the shops, his mother calling after him from the doorway—

"Watch yourself."

"It's okay, Ma."

The riots are over for a while. Tea time. A few teenagers in the gloom crouch behind burned out cars at the end of the road, smoking, balaclavas and slingshots in their hands, watching, waiting.

His sister Bridie runs out the door after him, rushing past her mother.

She cries out "Bridie! Bridie!"

The boy turns his head. A pale embryo of smoke escapes from a high recessed gun slit in the Saracen. He feels the velocity of the round displacing air near his face. The sound of it he feels still. The bullet hits Bridie on the bridge of her nose—lifts her off her feet—dashes her against the door lintel. Her face is blown asunder. Her brain tissue and blood streak down the wall of their house. A corrupt Belfast Passover.

Their mother screams.

He wants to scream himself but nothing comes out.

He stumbles back—his ragdoll sister lying broken.

Neighbors run out—pull the mother away.

Shrieking.

The Saracen indolently moves from its position, its underbelly exposed as it drives over the makeshift barricades of the Holy Land—Palestine Street, Jerusalem Street, Cairo Street. As it slowly moves off, the crowds are back out now. Stones cascade off the armor siding.

The priest arrives. The RUC arrive. Bridie's blood flows across the footpath, spilling over the lip, pooling on the warm summer roadway. The ambulance arrives. With ashen faces, they try to mop up the blood. They cover Bridie's face with a white sheet but mottled red stains spread quickly across the fabric. The boy walks over to stand beside Bridie's body.

His mother still screams, stricken, sirens cascading off the narrow gray streets as more ambulances and police cars arrive.

The boy looks down at the roadway. The bright black-red blood from his sister's head and nose and ears molding itself around his shoes and flowing on. He takes his shoes and socks off and stands in the warm blood so he won't forget.

The undertaker takes the body away to the Royal Victoria. The neighbors take their mother away. The boy's gaze follows the hearse before it disappears in the mist of the Ormeau Bridge. Neighbors try to persuade him to come indoors. He stands on the pavement until the night is high and the chill wind from the Lagan makes his knees shake. He walks into the house, tracking faint red blemishes on the linoleum in the hallway. In her bedroom, he pulls the sheet over his head. He lies awake all night.

In the morning, red footprints are embossed on the white sheet.

At the wake the next day, crowds flood the front parlor. The open coffin rests on hard backed kitchen chairs. Bridie's head wrapped with heavy white bandages. Whispers. Coughs. Blue-white cigarette smoke shrouds the mourners. Women in the kitchen pour drinks and tea and hand out ham sandwiches in muted silence.

The boy stands at the head of the coffin.

His mother hunched in the chair beside him vacantly staring ahead. The boy wears black trousers, white shirt and black tie. He stands there all day. He watches everyone in the room that approaches. Young, gaunt Boot Boys with sallow skin and fierce ferocious eyes nod at him. They touch his hand in passing, calloused hands, petrol tainted hands, joy-rider hands, stone thrower hands, skinny hands, lethal hands. He nods back.

He stands all night beside the coffin after his mother is taken to bed, when the neighbors drift home, when the relatives try to snatch sleep in the narrow bedrooms upstairs.

At the funeral, Bridie's classmates form a guard of honor as the cortege leaves the house for the church. Skinny pale legs and skinny pale faces, black ties and white shirts. The mass is full of weeping and God-redeeming.

The coffin is carried up the steep road from the church, the boy, his brother, and his cousins carrying Bridie. Her classmates walk alongside the coffin practicing the walk of sorrow, which they will soon bring to perfection.

ക

Every night from high rooftops the boy throws petrol bombs. He kisses each bottle before it flies end over end, the light cascading off it before it lands. He works quietly, efficiently. He went up to the roof for the first time the night of the funeral. His concentration is total. His throw is prodigious. Girls admire him. Kiss him. He waits until the Saracens are out of range of the other throwers.

Squaddies lean against the hard metal sides. Smoking. Laughing. Their rifles point to the ground. Relaxing.

Then the boy walks to the lip of the roof. He pulls petrol bombs from their crates. An acolyte lights them and then he throws. A wide flaming arc. The squaddies scatter, but too late. The bombs land true—melting skin into their khaki uniforms.

His mother watches him every time he leaves the house

and waits up until he comes home. Her sorrow burns deep. It is a fine, polished arc biting into him.

Outside the city, he is brought on long weekends when the sun is high in the summer sky and Catholics escape Belfast to the South, and in the fading evening he fires his revolver at targets in the windbreak trees of a safe house. The muzzle flash elegant, tapering into a jagged white corona of light twelve inches in front of the muzzle, the bullet cropping low-lying branches before hitting the cans and bottles in the shadows. The interval between shots is long as he lets the echoes of the gunfire dissipate before raising his arm again. When he fires a full chamber, he flicks the cylinder free in a practiced manner, the barrel pointed high into the air, letting the cartridges fall into his calloused hand and then dropping the warm casings into his pocket. With slow efficiency, he reloads and fires again, the night growing darker, the blossoms of gunfire growing whiter.

❧

He sits on the floor in an upstairs bedroom of a safe house in Ballymurphy, his back leaning against the wall covered with wallpaper of an Indian hunting party felling buffalo with lances and arrows, bareback on wild-looking horses flashing through tall prairie grass breathing down on the fleeing prey.

The window is open, catching the street sounds—Angelus bells, whoops from children playing in the long summer evening, the throb of army helicopters hovering over the Belfast streets.

Listening for footsteps coming up the path, listening for the laughs of local girls, listening for the English accents so admired and hated. A new pistol smuggled in from Spain with a patina of gun oil still clinging to the dull gray metal lies on the floor beside him. An older guy sits opposite him. To supervise him. To blood him, purge him.

The footfalls come up the path—girls laughing in the darkness.

Off-duty squaddies sprawling drunk on the couch in the sitting room. Relaxing. Revelers. A Friday night out in Belfast City—where the girls are pretty. Where things get fucking tricky. Where the Undertones played "Teenage Kicks" and Stiff Little Fingers played "Suspect Device" and the Outcasts played "Self-Conscious Over You." The music trying to push the hate disease back with the pogo, with staccato chords, with jagged rhythms. To push it back behind the barricades. Back into the clustered terraced houses where enmity seeped out for Brits or Prods or Taigs.

Girls from Republican families—fierce, fire-tried, fanatical—lure them in for the cause. For the kill. For brothers on hunger strike. For brothers shot dead by Paras. For brothers butchered by Prods. Fragile, febrile forever afterwards.

The squaddies had it coming.

Maybe.

Soldiers of the Realm.

Boys.

Boy soldiers.

Seventeen, eighteen, nineteen. Out!

Tough, working class youths plucked from the grim estates of Coventry, Manchester, Birmingham, Wolverhampton—pushed off to the even starker streets of Belfast. My beautiful, brash, beastly Belfast.

Protecting the Empire for White Hall mandarins with soft hands who took cream tea and played war games. Gloves off. The red hand of Ulster. Dipped in blood. No surrender. Fuck the Pope. Fuck the people. A strategic necessity, old chap!

Silently creeping down the stairs in runners, dry mouthed, bursting through into the sitting room.

Taken by surprise, the squaddies suddenly sober, anxious, youngsters only, two of them brothers. Cropped haircuts like the boy, unarmed, rising from the sofa, unsteady, "Teenage Kicks" playing.

The girls grab their bags, run out the path, pulling close the door behind them.

"Please, please!"

Silently the boy watches them, taking it in, the gun covering them, sweeping in small arcs, steady. The older man comes in behind the boy.

"Sorry lads," to them.

To the boy, "Do them."

Firing, aiming, some shots missing—hard to believe—a foot away. The squaddies fall, lie there, arms outstretched, quiver, bleed there.

A wee boy killer.

That boy was me.

News

The boy dreamed of flying, of diving, of jumping off buildings,
of falling through trap doors, of biplanes scanning the trenches of the
Western Front, of front-mounted machine guns firing through pro-
pellers, of the Hindenburg crashing in a fireball, of Messerschmidts
banking steeply away from bright arc lights, of Junkers and Heinkels
with fat payloads flying low on cold spring mornings, of the whine of
Stukas screaming down on railroad yards.

He felt hard knuckles along his spine, smacks to his head, his
ears ringing.

"Wake the fuck up."

His mother stood over him. It was dark still. He could see the red
glow from the cigarette.

"There's someone at the door. Take care of it."

❧

McGowan checked the window locks. He looked out on
St. Nicholas' Avenue and the Dominican Republic heartland
of Washington Heights. Nothing was amiss. Just the usual
filth. The bodegas full of toxic products from China, baker-
ies with cakes laced with sugar and starch, the street full of
garbage and fat pigeons and fat guys in shirt sleeves feeding
their fat counterparts as if pigeons were exotic pets.

Able-bodied Dominicans played dominoes on the side-
walk or lounged in hair salons where they admired themselves in ceiling-high mirrors and watched baseball for
hours on end. Indolent police patrols from the 85th Precinct
ambled by, talking on cell phones, scratching, busy as usual,
not paying attention except to the DR women bursting out

of nail shops and their blouses.

McGowan took consolation from the gray granite of the Catholic Church that abutted his building. At night, he went out his window and walked on the steep shining slates of the church roof and then up to the peak and along the ridge-line to the high granite cross where he looked down on the street.

The Irish were long gone since the church was built in 1930. Now the rural Irish accents were replaced with rapid-fire, harsh Spanish that European Spaniards loathed. There were almost no Irish within a mile radius of the five story walkup where McGowan lived. The only holdouts were in McGowan's building—John Kelly and his mother Eileen who was from Galway, McGowan's hometown. When they met on the stairs, she leaned on her cane and they talked about the Galway Races, the swans at Woodquay, the summer days when rain and sun fought with each other to get the upper hand, the fishing boats at the Claddagh, the lonesome sound of trawler diesel engines pulling out from the docks, the Promenade in Salthill, Claude's Casino, Griffin's tea rooms, Nimmo's, the Saturday morning market under the centuries old chestnut trees.

Eileen Kelly knew she wouldn't make it back to Galway, so had to remember every detail. McGowan knew he wouldn't go back. Sorrow leached through his days in Galway.

The Dominicans drove John Kelly crazy. Which wasn't hard. He was shell-shocked from Korea when a mortar round landed beside him in a waterlogged, shallow trench and blew four of his comrades asunder. His constant refrain now was, I wish it killed me too. He had a point, McGowan thought.

John banged on the floor with a hammer whenever the deep bass of house music vibrated from the apartment below. The Dominican who lived there, Hernandez, was a smalltime drug peddler and played music day and night.

McGowan didn't mind it so much. He liked rhythm. He liked sound. He liked vibration. He liked house. He liked order. He liked modulation. He liked tone. Plus, he wasn't shell-shocked from Korea or Belfast. McGowan only hated the dreadful merengue that the next door neighbor in 5C played on Saturday evenings as he entertained one of his many girlfriends. McGowan broke into 5C one day while the owner was out and stole the merengue collection. That night, he flung them Frisbee-like into the mile wide Hudson from the George Washington Bridge. The following Saturday, ABBA songs drifted through the walls.

At least it had some charm (French). And no Spanish.

One night after John Kelly's hammer crescendo reached a peak, Hernandez reached the tipping point. He raced upstairs and attacked the Kelly's door with his feet. When he saw the light appear through the spy-hole, he stabbed through the glass with an ice pick clutched tightly in his fist. It shattered the glass and kept going into Eileen Kelly's left eye (the good one). Blood and vitreous fluid squirted out and spread sluggishly down the shaft. The worse damage was done when he yanked the pick free from the spy-hole and fled downstairs. McGowan wasn't in that night.

He was over in Woodlawn taking care of someone.

The cops desolately investigated.

"Fuck—great—no witnesses except the blind old woman comatose in the hospital. That can be solved... like, never. You know who it is, John? Do you? Carlos Hernandez? Is that right? Well, fucking prove it."

End of investigation. The cops hated Kelly because he called the precinct every day about something. An eighty-year-old Irish woman didn't register high with the NYPD. If it was a buxom Dominican with a chipped nail they would be all business.

McGowan double-locked his door and walked down the stairs. The steps were stained from water damage and discarded cigarette butts. Upended cockroaches lay on the landing. He was hoping he would miss John Kelly but he heard the giveaway wheezes as John got nearer. McGowan usually had impeccable timing. At least when it counted. Climbing roofs, jumping bank counters, planning, scoping, waiting, escaping, taking care of things.

McGowan offered it up. Like a good, lapsed Irish Catholic.

John looked sicker than usual. He walked the George Washington Bridge every day for exercise and to get away from the Dominican hordes but it had little effect. He was pale and sickly. Now he kept vigil in the Columbia Presbyterian Hospital on 168th Street most of the day while his mother tried her best to die and get back to Galway for good. If it wasn't for his mother, he would have jumped off the bridge years ago. McGowan walked the bridge every night when John was safe inside. He looked down at the wide Hudson River and felt like flying over the parapet. He found it difficult to turn away and walk back to Manhattan when the deep space under the high struts of the bridge pulled him back.

John stopped in front of McGowan and began complaining about the music, the thugs, the animals, the pigs. The usual litany. When tenants passed them on the stairwell he increased the volume—pigs, animals, rats, scum, dogs, etcetera—so everyone could hear it. John watched them for a reaction. McGowan just nodded at the passing tenants and looked back at John until he eventually stopped. McGowan asked about his mother. The prognosis was poor. Even if she recovered, she would be as shell-shocked as John plus would need a patch for the hollowed-out eye socket. John nodded at McGowan and started up the last flight of stairs and stopped after two steps, turning.

"Any news for me yet?" the old man asked.

McGowan turned and headed down the stairs.

The street was full of double parked cars as Dominicans sat, music blaring from open windows, monitoring traffic wardens in rearview and side mirrors. They also watched Dominican women pass and made loud comments, sculpting with their hands elegant curves that were not always there.

The Dominicans casually appraised McGowan as usual—a white curiosity in the middle of merengue land. McGowan had the haunted look of the Irish in exile. He could have stayed in the Northern Irish enclave of Woodlawn but it reminded him of a cross between Athlone and Mullingar except no river where you could drown yourself.

McGowan walked ten blocks north to Inwood, scanning the crowds and the men lounging in chairs chained to stunted trees so they always had a place to sit. Talk about pre-planning. He spotted Hernandez, the ice-picker, sitting on the hood of a black Lincoln Continental. Smoking. Talking to other Dominican men. McGowan had to blend into the background but he had years of practice in Belfast. There were more whites in Inwood as well, which helped. McGowan strolled into a laundromat and watched Hernandez across the street. The whirr of dryers dulled the harsh, loud conversations going back and forth around him.

Hernandez eventually sloughed off the hood, did elaborate handshakes with the other Dominicans, and walked away down St. Nicholas. McGowan left the sudsy acrid pall of the laundromat. Halfway down the block, Hernandez walked into the foyer of a five story walkup. He rang the bell until the buzzer sounded. McGowan could hear it and waited a few seconds to quickly push in after him before the door clicked closed. Hernandez didn't notice. McGowan heard him clear his throat and spit on the landing above him. Charming. On the fourth floor, McGowan caught up with him. A cross breeze through the open windows cooled the landings.

The Dominican was sweating. McGowan was not. McGowan could see the moisture beaded on his forehead. He was looking out the window. He leaned out the window with his hands on the sill watching a woman in the neigh-

139

boring apartment building. McGowan walked behind him as if to pass and bent down and cut the Achilles tendons of both legs—an old Irish trick. Hernandez toppled backwards trying to grab the back of his legs with both hands which the severed tendons rendered useless. McGowan held him up and pulled him around so their faces met. Hernandez watched him in shock, his body bent over, his hands still trying to negate the loss of power in his legs. McGowan patted him down and pulled a silver ice-pick from a jacket pocket.

"You have a penchant for these, I see. That's French."

McGowan head-butted him in the nose. The cartilage snapped. Blood burst out. His eyes streamed with tears.

"Voluez-vous this?" McGowan pierced the Dominican's left eardrum with the slim stainless-steel point of the pick.

Then he did the other ear.

McGowan pulled the pick free.

"House that?"

Hernandez sagged against McGowan and he held him away as he started to vomit. Now Hernandez was holding a hand over each ear. Blood seeped between his fingers, dripping on the wooden floor. An upended cockroach was carried over the lip of the first step by the blood.

McGowan forced him backward toward the open window.

"Por favor!"

At last he seemed to recognize McGowan from their building. He was crying real tears now. Snot, tears and blood flowed down his chin. Viral city, McGowan thought.

McGowan pushed him back further. His head broke the glass of the upper pane. The woman in the adjoining building looked over. McGowan held Hernandez away from the window. She soon lost interest.

"Slan leat," (bye now) McGowan said and pushed him through the open window. The cry was cut short by the low heavy thud as the body hit the unyielding metal of the fire-escape. McGowan felt the vibration.

A sharp female cry rose from the street. He heard it before. McGowan walked down the stairs into the humid August day.

Now he had news for John.

Another One

"Where is he?"

"Upstairs."

"Okay."

I followed the man. My legs hurt.

I was tired.

I was tired every day now—tired of the daily interrogations, the calls in the middle of the night, the safe houses, culvert bombings, tripwires, helicopters hovering over us, bullets ricocheting off hard concrete, premature explosions, sniper bullets cutting necks in two, baton rounds pulverizing children's faces, blood flowing on the wet tarmac, the deathly graceful contours of AKs and Armalites.

I was tired of bodies in ditches, in back alleys, in front gardens, in playgrounds, in schoolyards, in churches, in Long Kesh, in Ballymurphy, in the Falls, in the Shankill, in South Armagh, in body bags, in shallow graves, in high rise apartments, in fish shops, in sweet shops.

My eyes were sore from the smoke of burned out cars and buildings, the sharp taint of long dispersed tear gas. I was sick of the smell of petrol bombs and the smell of fear. This lingered the longest.

I recognized the guy minding the door. I knew him from the Falls. He briefed me. It looked bad. Another one.

"We caught him red-handed."

"Okay."

He opened the door for me. I looked into his eyes before I stepped in.

The prisoner was slumped on a chair with a hood over his face. His head lay on the table top. Narrow rivulets of blood leaked out from under the hood and dripped over the edge of the table to the floor in beautiful, beastly drops.

I told the minder in the room to take the hood off and leave.

He did. The prisoner's face was black and blue and pulverized all over. Lump hammers do that. Both eyes were shut. Clumps of hair were missing. I noticed them on the floor when I sat down. There were cigarettes burns on his cheeks like malignant beauty spots. His nose was broken. Every time he breathed small bubbles of frothy blood appeared on his nostrils.

His mother wouldn't recognize him. His wife wouldn't recognize him. His children wouldn't recognize him. He probably wouldn't even recognize himself.

The sharp acrid smell of urine made me want to vomit.

I undid the gag on his mouth. It smelled bad. Saliva and drool spooled on the table. I wiped it off with his shirt sleeve, but the blood on his shirt streaked the table. That's just fucking great. I felt like yelling. I felt like fucking him out the window.

He tried to scream but nothing came out.

I knew how he felt.

Goodbye Sean

I was the first grandson but he was the handsomest.

Every August, my family escaped Galway on our holidays to my grandmother's farm in Renbrack. My cousin Sean called over, tramping across fields of long grass to greet us on our first day. His strong physique honed by farm work assailed my own city-pampered body. His strong rural accent assailed my urban, sanitized one. My grandmother watched him from the back kitchen, admiring him. Jealousy and anguish scraped against me.

I mocked his thick country accent and his rough ways. His physicality and rapture in the world mocked my own timid grasp on reality. His exuberance was steadfast and natural and it unnerved me—displacing my vectors of normality.

His strong body didn't protect him in the end though from a cancer that ate away the soft vulnerable tissue under his armpit and spread through the rich seam of capillaries and vessels that carried the germ to his young organs.

When he died, I cried hard.

☙

Our favorite pastime during those summer holidays was taking my uncle's pistol from his car while he slept late into the morning. Uncle Jack played football and handball and all night cards. And at being a detective. His service revolver was hidden under the back seat of his white Volkswagen Beetle, which had a patina of red etched into the frame by some obscure, irreversible weathering process. He hit a

144

sheep one night as he drove home through narrow, winding back roads as the mist shrouded the hills and rain cascaded off the windscreen and bonnet. I imagined the stain was the blood of an informer we had executed on one of the bohreens that crisscrossed the valley around us.

Myself and Sean lay in wait for neighbors passing the road, rushing out in front of them with the pistol leveled, demanding "Who goes there?" or asking for money with menaces or checking if they were Black and Tans or informers. They were tolerant and played along. They couldn't call the police because we were the police—or at least uncle Jack was.

We performed mock executions on the summer-warmed blacktop country roads, taking turns lying sprawled and still, breathing in the bituminous vapors. The executioner checked the body by turning the victim over with his foot. We strived for authenticity. Sometimes the coup de grace was delivered and the metal against your neck was a shock.

On other days, we re-enacted executions on the bog land near the house, toppling onto the soft loamy peat to lie staring without blinking at the narrow sliver of bog cotton in our line of vision.

On our days off from executions, we played hide and seek. We lay in high overgrown grass and listened while our siblings searched for us. We didn't move for hours. The only thing we could see through the undergrowth was each other's eyes and the unspoken communication between us was that we were different. We could outwait the others. We could endure. He admired me for this and I was glad.

Some days we pretended we were Indians and tied our siblings to telegraph poles and lit kindling, hay and heather under their feet. It was usually my brother we picked and once I couldn't release him in time and his shoes (or should that be moccasins) caught fire and he started shouting and crying. I eventually got the fire out. My brother was shocked and ran home slightly smoldering. He soon developed fire-starting tendencies and caused the great fire of Galway which burned for three days and nights, streaking through the docks and timber yards until it was stopped by the granite of the Great Southern Hotel. Later, he went to college to study medicine and forensic psychiatry and was happy dealing with people more traumatized than himself.

When the sun was as hot as an Irish summer sun can manage, we lay on our backs on the rough stubble of the hay fields and shaded our eyes from the sun. Sean talked about football and fighting and Boot Boys from Castlebar and the weather and fallow fields and the FCA and heifers and bullocks and fucking milk quotas and girls while I tried to assimilate any of it. Now and again, he would sit up and look at me as if my non-responsiveness was a curiosity that deserved attention but he never addressed it and just lay back down again and hummed tunes by The Indians or continued on another conversational tangent.

His self-confidence disturbed me. I became silent and fearful by his embracing of life, while every part of my own body struggled to stay calm. I couldn't find any aspect of my life that compared favorably to his.

When we lay on the banks of the Moy, our feet dangling in the water, pulled by the heft of the cooling fast flowing water, we shared a silence that is hard to articulate. The faint barks of dogs from across the river in Lismorane soothed us. The distant hum of cars on the roads across the river lulled us. Boys I knew had died in that river. Boys leaping in graceful arcs from the bridge at Toomore, boys splitting their heads on the sharp hidden rocks, boys slipping silently at dusk into the deep, deep channel. Boys like me.

Our last August together, we smoked cigarettes at dusk lying on heather covered rocks (note—perfect ambush terrain). High beam headlights from cars on the Foxford road reached out to us intermittently through swaying trees that sheltered us from the night chill. I wanted the smoke of his cigarette to damage the perfect skin of his face. Maybe this mental germ of mine sparked the cancer germ which destroyed his body. Sometimes I worry about that. I never meant it.

✲

I can still feel the coffin as I carried it with his brothers from the church. I still recall the Mayo rain on my face and the strong drizzle fogging my glasses, droplets forming on the varnished wood of the lid. The rain hid my tears. The silver handles were slippery and I worried about losing my grip. I can still hear the low vibration from the engine and the smell of diesel exhaust as we walked slowly behind the hearse. His three sisters walked in front of us, dressed in black, leaning against each other, their bodies frail and fatigued after weeks of night vigils. Sometimes they looked back at us and I watched their eyes and expressions through the crosshairs of heads and shoulders.

I remember the engine vibrating more strongly as we started on the steep hill leading from the town to the graveyard. Neighbors and friends stood on the grass verge, removing their caps as the coffin passed, a strong impulse of respect. These small farmers gave a more solemn blessing and acknowledgment than any church service. For the last few yards, his three sisters joined us to carry the coffin. They reminded me of the sisters of hunger strikers in Belfast carrying the desiccated remains of their fathers and sons to Milltown cemetery.

When we reached the gate, people came to shake hands with us. I felt like an interloper who had no right to be there and it triggered again my fear that my childhood envy had been made lethally manifest.

✲

Later that night, as family and neighbors drank Powers whiskey and bitter black tea, I walked out the back door then through the fields from their house to the graveyard. Dogs barked warnings in the distance. Black, rain-filled clouds rushed overhead blocking out the moon. The wind carried the promise of rain. When I got to Sean's grave I took the pistol from my jacket pocket. I fired six rounds into the air, the corona of white flashes from the muzzle blinding me. Rooks scattered in black clouds from the treeline above the cemetery, protesting, calling sharply.

I could only find some of the cartridges on the ground before I left him there.

On Her Birthday

He left Belfast around two in the morning.

Light traffic.

He liked driving at night... no school runs, no rush hour, no old people stopped at junctions bewildered by the lights and traffic, only a black Opel Vectra sailing through the seas of the dark, pulling in the miles, the wind buffeting the chassis, wipers scooping aside the heavy rain from the windscreen into the surrounding dark edges, the soothing hum of tires against the wet asphalt, the oncoming lights flooding the interior of the car, scanning him, the machine to machine pull as they speed past, disappearing into the rain and darkness, taillights fading splashes of blood in the rearview mirror, the vectors of sound and speed and direction intersecting with the blurred dark contours of hedges and stone walls and trees.

The disembodied reflection of the dashboard's dials keeps pace outside, banking, stopping, flying onward. Cold night air through a narrow gap at the top of the driver's window stings his face, keeps him alert, the whistling sound a lament.

Past Newry, squaddies prone against hedgerows and stone walls, following him in their scopes, fingers stiff from the rain and wind. High observation towers bathe the road in shocking strobe lights. Safe into the Irish Republic he breathes easier, then through Ardee and the lush pastureland of Navan and Trim. Forts, castles and monastic sites, woods, graveyards, schoolyards, church steeples, grottos to the Virgin Mary, cattle lying under elm trees.

Along narrow secondary roads to the main Dublin to Galway route, the macadam skin cracked in places and pushed up by the peat land so the car bounces over the uneven surface, a satisfying surge through his belly, a satisfying humph when it lands and skims onwards. Onward past Athlone, past a slippery junction where he crashed years before, skidding across black macadam greasy with rain and leaves, smacking into a boulder, skittering into a tributary road. Images and memories of near-death written in a past notation he can't decipher. The hieroglyphs of near-death etched on him forever.

Past Ballinasloe, bandit country in the eighteenth century where highwaymen on black horses waited in the shelter and cover of tall Irish oaks, a brace of pistols drawn, bundled in black long coat and tricorn hat, listening for the sound of high rimmed wheels against rough roadway, breath from their horses' nostrils smoking the air, rushing out from cover to strike at mail cars, landlords, and magistrates.

Near dawn he drove into Galway, in past the docks, the heavy heft of straining diesel engines from Atlantic-bound trawlers reaching him through the open window, their yellow cabin lights pale and diffuse, obscured by low lying mists rising off the sea, the smell of salt water soothing him.

Out past Salthill, past Claude Toft's casino, the Prom, the hills of Clare obscured, rain-heavy low black clouds out in Galway Bay promising showers, swelling waves bursting on the defense wall of the Prom, shattered fronds thrown up on the road like dismembered children's limbs. Past the Crescent, home of doctors and architects, whose sophisticated daughters in Taylor's Hill uniforms looked at him in disdain once. Past Palmyra Avenue where the teenage William Joyce lived until the IRA waited for him one dark evening in the shade of trees on Saint Mary's Road to shoot him. Past the Regional Hospital where once he lay dying, watching dusk fall, but fought back. Fought back from the dark, from the deep.

Around Eyre Square defiled forever where he lay once on the long grass in the summer when life was easy, when life eased off him at the end of the day. Not anymore.

Dawn now and he drove down the street. The house looked the same. He sat watching it for a long time, the water in Lough Atalia reflecting back the low clouds. He stepped out. Memories and emotions towered over him, fell down on him, fetching him back to here.

Inside the house, the wallpaper was mottled with age, the colors fading, leaching away now, the rooms quiet. The piano in the front room stood in shadow, sheathed in a cover of dust. On the mantelpiece were framed photos of his parents on their wedding day, monochrome print, suits, no wedding dress, both handsome, both destroyed now.

His father dead, his mother failing.

He pulled the door behind him and drove out to Athenry, to the nursing home. It was still early morning. The mist clung to the fields. The sun outlined the webs of dew created in the night. He drove up the long avenue to the front door of the home.

He saw her at the glass door staring out.

She waved.

She waved at everyone.

He had seen her once-lustrous intelligence ravaged. Had seen her washing her hands in the toilet bowl. Heard her crying at night. Felt her heart beating in panic when she startled awake and cried out. Listened at the foot of the stairs while she murmured her prayers in Irish. Listened to her random chatter of inconsequential matters.

He got out of the car. Reached the door and pushed his face up against the glass.

The occupants moved back in alarm.

Since he had an archipelago of wounds and stitches from eye to ear, it was not surprising. He didn't look his best. A ricocheting baton round in the Falls hit the gable end of a house and struck him. Crowd control, allegedly. That pint of milk he was carrying home for the tea was obviously suspect.

Forty stitches it took, but he kept the eye. It was bloodshot and pinched closed by the deeply bruised, black-red tissues.

His mother pressed her face against his on the opposite side of the glass. She didn't seem to mind his looks.

He rang the bell and the nurse appeared.

She kind of jumped when she saw his distorted face.

She opened it and said hello.

"You're here to take May out for her birthday?"

"No, we are going to the prom," he said.

She didn't laugh. She looked at him.

He looked back with what he had.

"Okay, May," she said in a sweeter voice. "Have a nice day out."

The nurse gave her a hug and held her hand as she passed her over.

They treated his mother well here... he broke in one night to check up. He knew they liked her because she still thought she was a nurse and would help them make beds. She did the ward round with the matron every morning as if she was in her training days again in nursing school in England.

His mother touched the puckered tissue around his eye socket and examined it with a professional look. It was the only tenderness he got anymore. She was one of the few people who didn't recoil at the creased skin and suture marks threading their way from ear to eye.

"What happened, Paddy?"

Paddy was her brother. Long gone. Long a favorite.

"Nothing, Ma. It's fine," he said.

"You should mind your eyes. Try Optrex."

"Okay, Ma."

He walked her arm-in-arm to the car. He looked back and waved at the other patients.

Some waved and some frowned and some stared like malevolent watchdogs.

She tried to sit in the driver's seat.

He had to persuade her to go in the passenger side.

He had to buckle her up since she lost this ability years ago. He turned on *Morning Ireland* for her.

"Hi, Ma. It's me... Jimmy," he said.

"Hello Jimmy."

"Do you remember me, Ma?" he said.

"You're Paddy?"

She forgets everything.

She forgets her childhood, and how she walked barefoot across the fields from Renbrack to Callow school, how she would lie in the shade on summer days and watch her father save hay, how she once knocked a pot of boiling water from the range that melted the skin off her back. She forgets her adolescence too, and the story of her friend Winnie Battle dying alone in the river field. She forgets the years she spent nursing in the open TB wards in Dublin and cycling through the hard rain to dress wounds of working class Galwegians.

She forgets his name... her first born.

McGowan sped down the driveway so he wouldn't have to think too much.

He was bringing her to Callow Lake near where she grew up. At tight bends she squirmed and protested.

"Slow down for Jaysus' sake!"

McGowan threatened to blindfold her. She laughed. She could get jokes, which was strange, but that's all she got. She touched the bruised tissue again.

"What happened, Paddy?"

"It's nothing, Ma."

"You should mind your eyes."

"Should I try Optrex?"

"Yes, Optrex is great."

They drove through Tuam and took the road to Claremorris. The sun was warm after the night's rain. The scent

153

from the hedgerows and fields intensified as the day got warmer. They stopped for ice cream after fifty miles—she did pretty well, but he had to intervene at times to make sure it didn't dribble down her dress, not to mention the beautiful upholstery of the black Opel Vectra.

When they got to Callow Lake, the August sun was warm, not scorching like a New York August. Dogs barked across the valley in the far-away farms of Renbrack, the hum of cars on the distant road a mantra. The lake surface was dark blue, like the iris of his one good eye. The wind coming over Cullneachtain smelt of heather and cut grass and turf smoke. The wind produced ripples on the lake surface. They went arm-in-arm down to the landing.

She put her feet in the water—he got her shoes off just in time.

Teenagers with tanned bodies jumped from a rocky outcrop.

She sat there looking across the lake.

"Do you remember this place?" he asked her.

"I remember being happy."

She started crying.

He looked away in case she saw him. He could still cry from both tear ducts. How is this fair? he thought.

They stayed all day. They ate food he brought and walked around the lake. She even lay on an outcrop of rock and slept for a while in the sun. Sleep smoothed her worry frowns.

Near dusk they had tea.

"I'm tired, Paddy," she said. "Can I go home now?"

"Soon, Ma."

He stroked her forehead. Her wild Irish hair felt like the rough gorse bushes all around them.

When her breathing slowed into a steady rhythm, he carried her in his arms down to the car.

The August sun slipped away over the hills of Cullneachtain.

Behind them, Callow Lake was a black pool.

CPSIA information can be obtained at www.ICGtesting.com
Printed in the USA
LVOW12s1918310713

345621LV00008B/618/P